William Archer, Alexander Lange Kielland

Tales of Two Countries

William Archer, Alexander Lange Kielland

Tales of Two Countries

ISBN/EAN: 9783337073824

Printed in Europe, USA, Canada, Australia, Japan

Cover: Foto ©Andreas Hilbeck / pixelio.de

More available books at **www.hansebooks.com**

ALEXANDER KIELLAND

Tales of Two Countries

Translated from the Norwegian by
WILLIAM ARCHER. With an In-
troduction by H. H. BOYESEN

NEW YORK
HARPER AND BROTHERS, PUBLISHERS
1891

CONTENTS.

INTRODUCTION.

In June, 1867, about a hundred enthusiastic youths were vociferously celebrating the attainment of the baccalaureate degree at the University of Norway. The orator on this occasion was a tall, handsome, distinguished-looking young man named Alexander Kielland, from the little coast-town of Stavanger. There was none of the crudity of a provincial either in his manners or his appearance. He spoke with a quiet self-possession and a pithy incisiveness which were altogether phenomenal.

"That young man will be heard from one of these days," was the unanimous verdict of those who listened to his clear-cut and finished sentences, and noted the maturity of his opinions.

But ten years passed, and outside of Stavanger no one ever heard of Alexander Kielland. His friends were aware that he had studied law, spent some winters in France, married, and settled himself as a dignitary in

his native town. It was understood that he
had bought a large brick and tile factory, and
that, as a manufacturer of these useful articles,
he bid fair to become a provincial magnate, as
his fathers had been before him. People had
almost forgotten that great things had been
expected of him; and some fancied, perhaps,
that he had been spoiled by prosperity. Remembering him, as I did, as the most brilliant
and notable personality among my university
friends, I began to apply to him Malloch's epigrammatic damnation of the man of whom it
was said at twenty that he would do great
things, at thirty that he might do great things,
and at forty that he might have done great
things.

This was the frame of mind of those who
remembered Alexander Kielland (and he was
an extremely difficult man to forget), when in
the year 1879 a modest volume of "novelettes" appeared, bearing his name. It was,
to all appearances, a light performance, but it
revealed a sense of style which made it, nevertheless, notable. No man had ever written
the Norwegian language as this man wrote it.
There was a lightness of touch, a perspicacity,
an epigrammatic sparkle and occasional flashes
of wit, which seemed altogether un-Norwegian.

It was obvious that this author was familiar with the best French writers, and had acquired through them that clear and crisp incisiveness of utterance which was supposed, hitherto, to be untransferable to any other tongue.

As regards the themes of these "novelettes" (from which the present collection is chiefly made up), it was remarked at the time of their first appearance that they hinted at a more serious purpose than their style seemed to imply. Who can read, for instance, "Pharaoh" (which in the original is entitled "A Ball Mood") without detecting the revolutionary note which trembles quite audibly through the calm and unimpassioned language? There is, by-the-way, a little touch of melodrama in this tale which is very unusual with Kielland. "Romance and Reality," too, is glaringly at variance with the conventional romanticism in its satirical contrasting of the pre-matrimonial and the post-matrimonial view of love and marriage. The same persistent tendency to present the wrong side as well as the right side—and not, as literary good-manners are supposed to prescribe, ignore the former—is obvious in the charming tale "At the Fair," where a little spice of wholesome truth spoils the thoughtlessly festive mood; and the squalor, the want, the envy, hate, and greed which prudence and a regard for business compel the performers to disguise to the public, become the more cruelly visible to the visitors of the little alley-way at the rear of the tents. In "A Good Conscience" the satirical note has a still more serious ring; but the same admirable self-re-straint which, next to the power of thought and expression, is the happiest gift an au-thor's fairy godmother can bestow upon him, saves Kielland from saying too much—from enforcing his lesson by marginal comments, *à la* George Eliot. But he must be obtuse, indeed, to whom this reticence is not more eloquent and effective than a page of philo-sophical moralizing.

"Hope's Clad in April Green" and "The Battle of Waterloo" (the first and the last tale in the Norwegian edition), are more untinged with a moral tendency than any of the forego-ing. The former is a mere *jeu d'esprit*, full of good-natured satire on the calf-love of very young people, and the amusing over-estimate of our importance to which we are all, at that age, peculiarly liable.

As an organist with vaguely-melodious hints foreshadows in his prelude the musical *motifs*

which he means to vary and elaborate in his
fugue, so Kielland lightly touched in these
"novelettes" the themes which in his later
works he has struck with a fuller volume and
power. What he gave in this little book was
a light sketch of his mental physiognomy, from
which, perhaps, his horoscope might be cast
and his literary future predicted.

Though an aristocrat by birth and training,
he revealed a strong sympathy with the toiling masses. But it was a democracy of the
brain, I should fancy, rather than of the heart.
As I read the book, twelve years ago, its tendency puzzled me considerably, remembering,
as I did, with the greatest vividness, the fastid-
ious and elegant personality of the author. I
found it difficult to believe that he was in earnest. The book seemed to me to betray the
whimsical *sans-culottism* of a man of pleasure
who, when the ball is at an end, sits down with
his gloves on and philosophizes on the arti-
ficiality of civilization and the wholesomeness
of honest toil. An indigestion makes him a
temporary communist; but a bottle of seltzer
presently reconciles him to his lot, and restores
the equilibrium of the universe. He loves the
people at a distance, can talk prettily about
the sturdy son of the soil, who is the core and

marrow of the nation, etc.; but he avoids contact with him, and, if chance brings them into
contact, he loves him with his handkerchief to
his nose.

I may be pardoned for having identified Alexander Kielland with this type with which I
am very familiar; and he convinced me, presently, that I had done him injustice. In his
next book, the admirable novel *Garman and
Worse*, he showed that his democratic proclivities were something more than a mood. He
showed that he took himself seriously, and he
compelled the public to take him seriously.
The tendency which had only flashed forth
here and there in the "novelettes" now revealed its whole countenance. The author's
theme was the life of the prosperous *bour-
geoisie* in the western coast-towns; he drew
their types with a hand that gave evidence of
intimate knowledge. He had himself sprung
from one of these rich ship-owning, patrician
families, had been given every opportunity to
study life both at home and abroad, and had
accumulated a fund of knowledge of the world,
which he had allowed quietly to grow before
making literary drafts upon it. The same
Gallic perspicacity of style which had charmed
in his first book was here in a heightened de-

gree; and there was, besides, the same under-
lying sympathy with progress and what is
called the ideas of the age. What mastery
of description, what rich and vigorous colors
Kielland had at his disposal was demonstrated
in such scenes as the funeral of Consul Garman and the burning of the ship. There
was, moreover, a delightful autobiographical
note in the book, particularly in boyish experiences of Gabriel Garman. Such things
no man invents, however clever; such material
no imagination supplies, however fertile. Except Fritz Reuter's Stavenhagen, I know no
small town in fiction which is so vividly and
completely individualized, and populated with
such living and credible characters. Take,
for instance, the two clergymen, Archdeacon
Sparre and the Rev. Mr. Martens, and it is not
necessary to have lived in Norway in order to
recognize and enjoy the faithfulness and the
artistic subtlety of these portraits. If they
have a dash of satire (which I will not under-
take to deny), it is such delicate and well-bred
satire that no one, except the originals, would
think of taking offence. People are willing,
for the sake of the entertainment which it
affords, to forgive a little quiet malice at
their neighbors' expense. The members of

the provincial bureaucracy are drawn with the same firm but delicate touch, and everything has that beautiful air of reality which proves the world akin.

It was by no means a departure from his previous style and tendency which Kielland signalized in his next novel, *Laboring People* (1881). He only emphasizes, as it were, the heavy, serious bass chords in the composite theme which expresses his complex personality, and allows the lighter treble notes to be momentarily drowned. Superficially speaking, there is perhaps a reminiscence of Zola in this book, not in the manner of treatment, but in the subject, which is the corrupting influence of the higher classes upon the lower. There is no denying that in spite of the ability, which it betrays in every line, *Laboring People* is unpleasant reading. It frightened away a host of the author's early admirers by the uncompromising vigor and the glaring realism with which it depicted the consequences of vicious indulgence. It showed no consideration for delicate nerves, but was for all that a clean and wholesome book.

Kielland's third novel, *Skipper Worse*, marked a distinct step in his development. It was less of a social satire and more of a social study.

It was not merely a series of brilliant, exqui-
sitely-finished scenes, loosely strung together
on a slender thread of narrative, but it was a
concise and well-constructed story, full of beautiful scenes and admirable portraits.   The
theme is akin to that of Daudet's *L'Evangé-
liste ;* but Kielland, as it appears to me, has in
this instance outdone his French *confrère* as
regards insight into the peculiar character and
poetry of the pietistic movement. He has
dealt with it as a psychological and not pri-
marily as a pathological phenomenon. A com-
parison with Daudet suggests itself constantly
in reading Kielland. Their methods of work-
manship and their attitude towards life have
many points in common. The charm of style,
the delicacy of touch and felicity of phrase, is in
both cases pre-eminent. Daudet has, however,
the advantage (or, as he himself asserts, the dis-
advantage) of working in a flexible and highly-
finished language, which bears the impress of
the labors of a hundred masters; while Kielland
has to produce his effects of style in a poorer and
less pliable language, which often pants and
groans in its efforts to render a subtle thought.
To have polished this tongue and sharpened
its capacity for refined and incisive utterance
is one—and not the least—of his merits.

Though he has by nature no more sympathy with the pietistic movement than Daudet, Kielland yet manages to get, psychologically, closer to his problem. His pietists are more humanly interesting than those of Daudet, and the little drama which they set in motion is more genuinely pathetic. Two superb figures—the lay preacher, Hans Nilsen, and Skipper Worse—surpass all that the author had hitherto produced, in depth of conception and brilliancy of execution. The marriage of that delightful, profane old sea-dog Jacob Worse, with the pious Sara Torvested, and the attempts of his mother-in-law to convert him, are described, not with the merely superficial drollery to which the subject invites, but with a sweet and delicate humor, which trembles on the verge of pathos.

The beautiful story *Elsie*, which, though published separately, is scarcely a full-grown novel, is intended to impress society with a sense of responsibility for its outcasts. While Björnstjerne Björnson is fond of emphasizing the responsibility of the individual to society, Kielland chooses by preference to reverse the relation. The former (in his remarkable novel *Flags are Flying in City and Harbor*) selects a hero with vicious inherited tendencies, re-

deemed by wise education and favorable environment; the latter portrays in Elsie a hero-
ine with no corrupt predisposition, destroyed
by the corrupting environment which society
forces upon those who are born in her circumstances. Elsie could not be good, because
the world is so constituted that girls of her
kind are not expected to be good. Temptations, perpetually thronging in her way, break
down the moral bulwarks of her nature. Resistance seems in vain. In the end there is
scarcely one who, having read her story, will
have the heart to condemn her.

Incomparably clever is the satire on the be-
nevolent societies, which appear to exist as a
sort of moral poultice to tender consciences,
and to furnish an officious sense of virtue to
its prosperous members. "The Society for
the Redemption of the Abandoned Women
of St. Peter's Parish" is presided over by a
gentleman who privately furnishes subjects
for his public benevolence. However, as his
private activity is not bounded by the pre-
cincts of St. Peter's Parish, within which the
society confines its remedial labors, the miserable creatures who might need its aid are sent
away uncomforted. The delicious joke of the
thing is that "St. Peter's" is a rich and exclu-

sive parish, consisting of what is called "the better classes," and has no "abandoned women." Whatever wickedness there may be in St. Peter's is discreetly veiled, and makes no claim upon public charity. The virtuous horror of the secretary when she hears that the "abandoned woman" who calls upon her for aid has a child, though she is unmarried, is both comic and pathetic. It is the clean, "deserving poor," who understand the art of hypocritical humility—it is these whom the society seeks in vain in St. Peter's Parish.

Still another problem of the most vital consequence Kielland has attacked in his two novels, *Poison* and *Fortuna* (1884). It is, broadly stated, the problem of education. The hero in both books is Abraham Lövdahl, a well-endowed, healthy, and altogether promising boy who, by the approved modern educational process, is mentally and morally crippled, and the germs of what is great and good in him are systematically smothered by that disrespect for individuality and insistence upon uniformity, which are the curses of a small society. The revolutionary discontent which vibrates in the deepest depth of Kielland's nature; the profound and uncompromising radicalism which smoulders under his polished

exterior; the philosophical pessimism which
relentlessly condemns all the flimsy and superficial reformatory movements of the day, have
found expression in the history of the childhood, youth, and manhood of Abraham Lövdahl. In the first place, it is worthy of note
that to Kielland the knowledge which is of-
fered in the guise of intellectual nourishment
is poison. It is the dry and dusty accumula-
tion of antiquarian lore, which has little or no
application to modern life—it is this which the
young man of the higher classes is required to
assimilate. Apropos of this, let me quote Dr.
G. Brandes, who has summed up the tendency
of these two novels with great felicity:

"The author has surveyed the generation
to which he himself belongs, and after having
scanned these wide domains of emasculation,
these prairies of spiritual sterility, these vast
plains of servility and irresolution, he has ad-
dressed to himself the questions: How does a
whole generation become such? How was it
possible to nip in the bud all that was fertile
and eminent? And he has painted a picture
of the history of the development of the present generation in the home-life and school-life
of Abraham Lövdahl, in order to show from
what kind of parentage those most fortunately

situated and best endowed have sprung, and what kind of education they received at home and in the school. This is, indeed, a simple and an excellent theme.

" We first see the child led about upon the wide and withered common of knowledge, with the same sort of meagre fodder for all ; we see it trained in mechanical memorizing, in barren knowledge concerning things and forms that are dead and gone ; in ignorance concerning the life that is, in contempt for it, and in the consciousness of its privileged position, by dint of its possession of this doubtful culture. We see pride strengthened ; the healthy curiosity, the desire to ask questions, killed."

We are apt to console ourselves on this side of the ocean with the idea that these social problems appertain only to the effete monarchies of Europe, and have no application with us. But, though I readily admit that the keenest point of this satire is directed against the small States which, by the tyranny of the dominant mediocrity, cripple much that is good and great by denying it the conditions of growth and development, there is yet a deep and abiding lesson in these two novels which applies to modern civilization in gen-

eral, exposing glaring defects which are no
less prevalent here than in the Old World.

Besides being the author of some minor
comedies and a full-grown drama ("The Pro-
fessor"), Kielland has published two more novels, *St. John's Eve* (1887) and *Snow*. The latter
is particularly directed against the orthodox
Lutheran clergy, of which the Rev. Daniel
Jürges is an excellent specimen. He is, in
my opinion, not in the least caricatured; but
portrayed with a conscientious desire to do
justice to his sincerity. Mr. Jürges is a
worthy type of the Norwegian country pope,
proud and secure in the feeling of his divine
authority, passionately hostile to "the age,"
because he believes it to be hostile to Christ;
intolerant of dissent; a guide and ruler of
men, a shepherd of the people. The only
trouble in Norway, as elsewhere, is that the
people will no longer consent to be shepherd-
ed. They refuse to be guided and ruled.
They rebel against spiritual and secular authority, and follow no longer the bell-wether
with the timid gregariousness of servility and
irresolution. To bring the new age into the
parsonage of the reverend obscurantist in the
shape of a young girl—the *fiancée* of the pastor's son—was an interesting experiment which

B

gives occasion for strong scenes and, at last,
for a drawn battle between the old and the
new. The new, though not acknowledging itself to be beaten, takes to its heels, and flees
in the stormy night through wind and snow.
But the snow is moist and heavy; it is beginning to thaw. There is a vague presentiment
of spring in the air.

This note of promise and suspense with
which the book ends is meant to be symbolic.
From Kielland's point of view, Norway is yet
wrapped in the wintry winding-sheet of a
tyrannical orthodoxy; and all that he dares
assert is that the chains of frost and snow
seem to be loosening. There is a spring feeling in the air.

This spring feeling is, however, scarcely per-
ceptible in his last book, *Jacob*, which is written in anything but a hopeful mood. It is,
rather, a protest against that optimism which
in fiction we call poetic justice. The harsh
and unsentimental logic of reality is empha-
sized with a ruthless disregard of rose-colored
traditions. The peasant lad Wold, who, like
all Norse peasants, has been brought up on
the Bible, has become deeply impressed with
the story of Jacob, and God's persistent par-
tisanship for him, in spite of his dishonesty

and tricky behavior. The story becomes, half unconsciously, the basis of his philosophy of life, and he undertakes to model his career on that of the Biblical hero. He accordingly cheats and steals with a clever moderation, and in a cautious and circumspect manner which defies detection. Step by step he rises in the regard of his fellow-citizens; crushes, with long-headed calculation or with brutal promptness (as it may suit his purpose) all those who stand in his way, and arrives at last at the goal of his desires. He becomes a local magnate, a member of parliament, where he poses as a defender of the simple, old-fashioned orthodoxy, is decorated by the King, and is an object of the envious admiration of his fellow-townsmen.

From the pedagogic point of view, I have no doubt that *Jacob* would be classed as an immoral book. But the question of its morality is of less consequence than the question as to its truth. The most modern literature, which is interpenetrated with the spirit of the age, has a way of asking dangerous questions— questions before which the reader, when he perceives their full scope, stands aghast. Our old idyllic faith in the goodness and wisdom of all mundane arrangements has undoubtedly received a shock from which it will never recover. Our attitude towards the universe is changing with the change of its attitude towards us. What the thinking part of humanity is now largely engaged in doing is to readjust itself towards the world and the world towards it. Success is but a complete adaptation to environment; and success is the supreme aim of the modern man. The authors who, by their fearless thinking and speaking, help us towards this readjustment should, in my opinion, whether we choose to accept their conclusions or not, be hailed as benefactors. It is in the ranks of these that Alexander Kielland has taken his place, and now occupies a conspicuous position.

HJALMAR HJORTH BOYESEN.

NEW YORK, *May* 15, 1891.

PHARAOH.

PHARAOH.

SHE had mounted the shining marble steps without mishap, without labor, sustained by her great beauty and her fine nature alone. She had taken her place in the salons of the rich and great without paying for her admittance with her honor or her good name. Yet no one could say whence she came, though people whispered that it was from the depths.

As a waif of a Parisian faubourg, she had starved through her childhood among surroundings of vice and poverty, such as those only can conceive who know them by experience. Those of us who get our knowledge from books and from hearsay have to strain our imagination in order to form an idea of the hereditary misery of a great city, and yet our most terrible imaginings are apt to pale before the reality.

It had been only a question of time when vice should get its clutches upon her, as a cog-wheel seizes whoever comes too near the machine. After whirling her around through a short life of shame and degradation, it would, with mechanical punctu-

ality, have cast her off into some corner, there to
drag out to the end, in sordid obscurity, her carica-
ture of an existence.

But it happened, as it does sometimes happen,
that she was "discovered" by a man of wealth and
position, one day when, a child of fourteen, she
happened to cross one of the better streets. She
was on her way to a dark back room in the Rue
des Quatre Vents, where she worked with a woman
who made artificial flowers.

It was not only her extraordinary beauty that attracted her patron ; her movements, her whole bearing, and the expression of her half-formed features,
all seemed to him to show that here was an originally fine nature struggling against incipient corruption. Moved by one of the incalculable whims
of the very wealthy, he determined to try to rescue
the unhappy child.

It was not difficult to obtain control of her, as
she belonged to no one. He gave her a name, and
placed her in one of the best convent schools. Before long her benefactor had the satisfaction of observing that the seeds of evil died away and disappeared. She developed an amiable, rather indolent
character, correct and quiet manners, and a rare
beauty.

When she grew up he married her. Their married life was peaceful and pleasant : in spite of the
great difference in their ages, he had unbounded
confidence in her, and she deserved it.

Married people do not live in such close commu-
nion in France as they do with us; so that their
claims upon each other are not so great, and their
disappointments are less bitter.

She was not happy, but contented. Her character lent itself to gratitude. She did not feel the
tedium of wealth; on the contrary, she often took
an almost childish pleasure in it. But no one
could guess that, for her bearing was always full
of dignity and repose. People suspected that there
was something questionable about her origin, but
as no one could answer questions they left off asking them. One has so much else to think of in
Paris.

She had forgotten her past. She had forgotten
it just as we have forgotten the roses, the ribbons,
and faded letters of our youth—because we never
think about them. They lie locked up in a drawer
which we never open. And yet, if we happen now
and again to cast a glance into this secret drawer,
we at once notice if a single one of the roses,
or the least bit of ribbon, is wanting. For we
remember them all to a nicety; the memories
are as fresh as ever—as sweet as ever, and as
bitter.

It was thus she had forgotten her past—locked
it up and thrown away the key.

But at night she sometimes dreamed frightful
things. She could once more feel the old witch
with whom she lived shaking her by the shoulder,

and driving her out in the cold mornings to work at her artificial flowers.

Then she would jump up in her bed, and stare out into the darkness in the most deadly fear. But presently she would touch the silk coverlet and the soft pillows; her fingers would follow the rich carvings of her luxurious bed; and while sleepy little child-angels slowly drew aside the heavy dream-curtain, she tasted in deep draughts the peculiar, indescribable well-being we feel when we discover that an evil and horrible dream was a dream and nothing more.

.   .   .   .

Leaning back among the soft cushions, she drove to the great ball at the Russian ambassador's. The nearer they got to their destination the slower became the pace, until the carriage reached the regular queue, where it dragged on at a foot-pace.

In the wide square in front of the hôtel, brilliantly lighted with torches and with gas, a great crowd of people had gathered. Not only passers-by who had stopped to look on, but more especially workmen, loafers, poor women, and ladies of questionable appearance, stood in serried ranks on both sides of the row of carriages. Humorous remarks and coarse witticisms in the vulgarest Parisian dialect hailed down upon the passing carriages and their occupants.

She heard words which she had not heard for many years, and she blushed at the thought that she was perhaps the only one in this whole long line of carriages who understood these low expressions of the dregs of Paris.

She began to look at the faces around her: it seemed to her as if she knew them all. She knew what they thought, what was passing in each of these tightly-packed heads; and little by little a host of memories streamed in upon her. She fought against them as well as she could, but she was not herself this evening.

She had not, then, lost the key to the secret drawer; reluctantly she drew it out, and the memories overpowered her.

She remembered how often she herself, still almost a child, had devoured with greedy eyes the fine ladies who drove in splendor to balls or theatres; how often she had cried in bitter envy over the flowers she laboriously pieced together to make others beautiful. Here she saw the same greedy eyes, the same inextinguishable, savage envy.

And the dark, earnest men who scanned the equipages with half-contemptuous, half-threatening looks — she knew them all.

Had not she herself, as a little girl, lain in a corner and listened, wide-eyed, to their talk about the injustice of life, the tyranny of the rich, and the rights of the laborer, which he had only to reach out his hand to seize?

She knew that they hated everything—the sleek

horses, the dignified coachmen, the shining carriages, and, most of all, the people who sat within them—these insatiable vampires, these ladies, whose ornaments for the night cost more gold than any one of them could earn by the work of a whole lifetime.

And as she looked along the line of carriages, as it dragged on slowly through the crowd, another memory flashed into her mind—a half-forgotten picture from her school-life in the convent.

She suddenly came to think of the story of Pharaoh and his war-chariots following the children of Israel through the Red Sea. She saw the waves, which she had always imagined red as blood, piled up like a wall on both sides of the Egyptians.

Then the voice of Moses sounded. He stretched out his staff over the waters, and the Red Sea waves hurtled together and swallowed up Pharaoh and all his chariots.

She knew that the wall which stood on each side of her was wilder and more rapacious than the waves of the sea; she knew that it needed only a voice, a Moses, to set all this human sea in motion, hurling it irresistibly onward until it should sweep away all the glory of wealth and greatness in its blood-red waves.

Her heart throbbed, and she crouched trembling into the corner of the carriage. But it was not with fear; it was so that those without should not see her—for she was ashamed to meet their eyes.

For the first time in her life, her good-fortune appeared to her in the light of an injustice, a thing to blush for.

Was she in her right place, in this soft-cushioned carriage, among these tyrants and blood-suckers? Should she not rather be out there in the billowing mass, among the children of hate?

Half-forgotten thoughts and feelings thrust up their heads like beasts of prey which have long lain bound. She felt strange and homeless in her glittering life, and thought with a sort of demoniac longing of the horrible places from which she had risen.

She seized her rich lace shawl; there came over her a wild desire to destroy, to tear something to pieces; but at this moment the carriage turned into the gate-way of the hôtel.

The footman tore open the door, and with her gracious smile, her air of quiet, aristocratic distinction, she alighted.

A young attaché rushed forward, and was happy when she took his arm, still more enraptured when he thought he noticed an unusual gleam in her eyes, and in the seventh heaven when he felt her arm tremble.

Full of pride and hope, he led her with sedulous politeness up the shining marble steps.

.   .   .   .

"Tell me, *belle dame*, what good fairy endowed you in your cradle with the marvellous gift of transforming everything you touch into something new and strange. The very flower in your hair has a charm, as though it were wet with the fresh morning dew. And when you dance it seems as though the floor swayed and undulated to the rhythm of your footsteps."

The Count was himself quite astonished at this long and felicitous compliment, for as a rule he did not find it easy to express himself coherently. He expected, too, that his beautiful partner would show her appreciation of his effort.

But he was disappointed. She leaned over the balcony, where they were enjoying the cool evening air after the dance, and gazed out over the crowd and the still-advancing carriages. She seemed not to have understood the Count's great achievement; at least he could only hear her whisper the inex_plicable word, " Pharaoh."

He was on the point of remonstrating with her, when she turned round, made a step towards the salon, stopped right in front of him, and looked him in the face with great, wonderful eyes, such as the Count had never seen before.

" I scarcely think, Monsieur le Comte, that any good fairy—perhaps not even a cradle—was present at my birth. But in what you say of my flow-ers and my dancing your penetration has led you to a great discovery. I will tell you the secret of the fresh morning dew which lies on the flowers. It is the tears, Monsieur le Comte, which envy and shame, disappointment and remorse, have wept over them. And if you seem to feel the floor swaying as we dance, that is because it trembles under the hatred of millions."

She had spoken with her customary repose, and with a friendly bow she disappeared into the salon.

. . . .

The Count remained rooted to the spot. He cast a glance over the crowd outside. It was a sight he had often seen, and he had made sundry more or less trivial witticisms about the " many-headed monster." But to-night it struck him for the first time that this monster was, after all, the most unpleasant neighbor for a palace one could possibly imagine.

Strange and disturbing thoughts whirled in the brain of Monsieur le Comte, where they found plenty of space to gyrate. He was entirely thrown off his balance, and it was not till after the next polka that his placidity returned.

. . . .

THE PARSONAGE.

THE PARSONAGE.

IT seemed as though the spring would never come. All through April the north wind blew and the nights were frosty. In the middle of the day the sun shone so warmly that a few big flies began to buzz around, and the lark proclaimed, on its word of honor, that it was the height of summer.

But the lark is the most untrustworthy creature under heaven. However much it might freeze at night, the frost was forgotten at the first sunbeam; and the lark soared, singing, high over the heath, until it bethought itself that it was hungry.

Then it sank slowly down in wide circles, singing, and beating time to its song with the flickering of its wings. But a little way from the earth it folded its wings and dropped like a stone down into the heather.

The lapwing tripped with short steps among the hillocks, and nodded its head discreetly. It had no great faith in the lark, and repeated its wary "Bi litt! Bi litt!"* A couple of mallards lay snug-

---

*"Wait a bit! Wait a bit!" Pronounced *Bee leet*.

gling in a marsh-hole, and the elder one was of opinion that spring would not come until we had rain.

Far on into May the meadows were still yellow; only here and there on the sunny leas was there any appearance of green. But if you lay down upon the earth you could see a multitude of little shoots—some thick, others as thin as green darning-needles—which thrust their heads cautiously up through the mould. But the north wind swept so coldly over them that they turned yellow at the tips, and looked as if they would like to creep back again.

But that they could not do: so they stood still and waited, only sprouting ever so little in the midday sun.

The mallard was right; it was rain they wanted. And at last it came—cold in the beginning, but gradually warmer; and when it was over the sun came out in earnest. And now you would scarcely have known it again; it shone warmly, right from the early morning till the late evening, so that the nights were mild and moist.

Then an immense activity set in; everything was behindhand, and had to make up for lost time. The petals burst from the full buds with a little crack, and all the big and little shoots made a sudden rush. They darted out stalks, now to the one side, now to the other, as quickly as though they lay kicking with green legs. The meadows were

spangled with flowers and weeds, and the heather
slopes towards the sea began to light up.

Only the yellow sand along the shore remained
as it was; it has no flowers to deck itself with, and
lyme-grass is all its finery. Therefore it piles itself
up into great mounds, seen far and wide along the
shore, on which the long soft stems sway like a
green banner.

There the sand-pipers ran about so fast that their
legs looked like a piece of a tooth comb. The
sea-gulls walked on the beach, where the waves
could sweep over their legs. They held themselves
sedately, their heads depressed and their crops
protruded, like old ladies in muddy weather.

The sea-pie stood with his heels together, in his
tight trousers, his black swallow-tail, and his white
waistcoat.

" Til By'n! Til By'n !"* he cried, and at each cry
he made a quick little bow, so that his coat tails
whisked up behind him.

Up in the heather the lapwing flew about flapping her wings. The spring had overtaken her so
suddenly that she had not had time to find a proper place for her nest. She had laid her eggs right
in the middle of a flat-topped mound. It was all
wrong, she knew that quite well; but it could not
be helped now.

The lark laughed at it all; but the sparrows were
2

*" To town! to town !"

all in a hurry-scurry. They were not nearly ready. Some had not even a nest ; others had laid an egg or two ; but the majority had sat on the cow-house roof, week out, week in, chattering about the almanac.

Now they were in such a fidget they did not know where to begin. They held a meeting in a great rose-bush, beside the Pastor's garden-fence, all cackling and screaming together. The cock-sparrows ruffled themselves up, so that all their feathers stood straight on end ; and then they perked their tails up slanting in the air, so that they looked like little gray balls with a pin stuck in them. So they trundled down the branches and ricochetted away over the meadow.

All of a sudden, two dashed against each other. The rest rushed up, and all the little balls wound themselves into one big one. It rolled forward from under the bush, rose with a great hubbub a little way into the air, then fell in one mass to the earth and went to pieces. And then, without uttering a sound, each of the little balls suddenly went his way, and a moment afterwards there was not a sparrow to be seen about the whole Parsonage.

Little Ansgarius had watched the battle of the sparrows with lively interest. For, in his eyes, it was a great engagement, with charges and cavalry skirmishes. He was reading *Universal History* and the *History of Norway* with his father, and there-

fore everything that happened about the house
assumed a martial aspect in one way or another.
When the cows came home in the evening, they
were great columns of infantry advancing; the hens
were the volunteer forces, and the cock was Burgomaster Nansen.

Ansgarius was a clever boy, who had all his dates
at his fingers' ends; but he had no idea of the
meaning of time. Accordingly, he jumbled together
Napoleon and Eric Blood - Axe and Tiberius; and
on the ships which he saw sailing by in the offing
he imagined Tordenskiold doing battle, now with
Vikings, and now with the Spanish Armada.

In a secret den behind the summer-house he
kept a red broom-stick, which was called Bucephalus. It was his delight to prance about the garden with his steed between his legs, and a flower-
stick in his hand.

A little way from the garden there was a hillock
with a few small trees upon it. Here he could lie
in ambush and keep watch far and wide over the
heathery levels and the open sea.

He never failed to descry one danger or another
drawing near; either suspicious-looking boats on
the beach, or great squadrons of cavalry advancing
so cunningly that they looked like nothing but a
single horse. But Ansgarius saw through their
stealthy tactics; he wheeled Bucephalus about,
tore down from the mound and through the garden, and dashed at a gallop into the farm - yard.

The hens shrieked as if their last hour had come, and Burgomaster Nansen flew right against the Pastor's study window.

The Pastor hurried to the window, and just caught sight of Bucephalus's tail as the hero dashed round the corner of the cow-house, where he proposed to place himself in a posture of defence.

"That boy is deplorably wild," thought the Pastor. He did not at all like all these martial proclivities. Ansgarius was to be a man of peace, like the Pastor himself; and it was a positive pain to him to see how easily the boy learned and assimilated everything that had to do with war and fighting.

The Pastor would try now and then to depict the peaceful life of the ancients or of foreign nations. But he made little impression. Ansgarius pinned his faith to what he found in his book; and there it was nothing but war after war. The people were all soldiers, the heroes waded in blood; and it was fruitless labor for the Pastor to try to awaken the boy to any sympathy with those whose blood they waded in.

It would occur to the Pastor now and again that it might, perhaps, have been better to have filled the young head from the first with more peaceful ideas and images than the wars of rapacious monarchs or the murders and massacres of our forefathers. But then he remembered that he himself had gone through the same course in his boyhood

so that it must be all right. Ansgarius would be
a man of peace none the less—and if not! "Well,
everything is in the hand of Providence," said the
Pastor confidingly, and set to work again at his
sermon.

"You're quite forgetting your lunch to-day, father," said a blond head in the door-way.

"Why, so I am, Rebecca; I'm a whole hour too
late," answered the father, and went at once into
the dining-room.

The father and daughter sat down at the lunch-
eon-table. Ansgarius was always his own master
on Saturdays, when the Pastor was taken up with
his sermon.

You would not easily have found two people who
suited each other better, or who lived on terms of
more intimate friendship, than the Pastor and his
eighteen-year-old daughter. She had been motherless from childhood; but there was so much that
was womanly in her gentle, even-tempered father,
that the young girl, who remembered her mother
only as a pale face that smiled on her, felt the loss
rather as a peaceful sorrow than as a bitter pain.

And for him she came to fill up more and more,
as she ripened, the void that had been left in his
soul; and all the tenderness, which at his wife's
death had been so clouded in sorrow and longing,
now gathered around the young woman who grew
up under his eyes; so that his sorrow was assuaged
and peace descended upon his mind.

Therefore he was able to be almost like a mother to her. He taught her to look upon the world with his own pure, untroubled eyes. It became the better part of his aim in life to hedge her around and protect her fragile and delicate nature from all the soilures and perturbations which make the world so perplexing, so difficult, and so dangerous an abiding-place.

When they stood together on the hill beside the Parsonage, gazing forth over the surging sea, he would say: "Look, Rebecca! yonder is an image of life—of that life in which the children of this world are tossed to and fro; in which impure passions rock the frail skiff about, to litter the shore at last with its shattered fragments. He only can defy the storm who builds strong bulwarks around a pure heart—at his feet the waves break powerlessly."

Rebecca clung to her father; she felt so safe by his side. There was such a radiance over all he said, that when she thought of the future she seemed to see the path before her bathed in light. For all her questions he had an answer; nothing was too lofty for him, nothing too lowly. They exchanged ideas without the least constraint, almost like brother and sister.

And yet one point remained dark between them. On all other matters she would question her father directly; here she had to go indirectly to work, to get round something which she could never get over.

She knew her father's great sorrow; she knew what happiness he had enjoyed and lost. She followed with the warmest sympathy the varying fortunes of the lovers in the books she read aloud during the winter evenings; her heart understood that love, which brings the highest joy, may also cause the deepest sorrow. But apart from the sorrows of ill-starred love, she caught glimpses of something else—a terrible something which she did not understand. Dark forms would now and then appear to her, gliding through the paradise of love, disgraced and abject. The sacred name of love was linked with the direst shame and the deepest misery. Among people whom she knew, things happened from time to time which she dared not think about; and when, in stern but guarded words, her father chanced to speak of moral corruption, she would shrink, for hours afterwards, from meeting his eye.

He remarked this and was glad. In such sensitive purity had she grown up, so completely had he succeeded in holding aloof from her whatever could disturb her childlike innocence, that her soul was like a shining pearl to which no mire could cling.

He prayed that he might ever keep her thus!

So long as he himself was there to keep watch, no harm should approach her. And if he was called away, he had at least provided her with armor of proof for life, which would stand her in good stead on the day of battle. And a day of battle no doubt would come. He gazed at her with a look which she did not understand, and said with his strong faith, " Well, well, everything is in the hand of Providence !"

" Haven't you time to go for a walk with me to-day, father?" asked Rebecca, when they had finished dinner.

" Why, yes; do you know, I believe it would do me good. The weather is delightful, and I've been so industrious that my sermon is as good as finished."

They stepped out upon the threshold before the main entrance, which faced the other buildings of the farm. There was this peculiarity about the Parsonage, that the high-road, leading to the town, passed right through the farm-yard. The Pastor did not at all like this, for before everything he loved peace and quietness; and although the district was sufficiently out-of-the-way, there was always a certain amount of life on the road which led to the town.

But for Ansgarius the little traffic that came their way was an inexhaustible source of excitement. While the father and daughter stood on the threshold discussing whether they should follow the road or go through the heather down to the beach, the young warrior suddenly came rushing up the hill and into the yard. He was flushed and out of breath, and Bucephalus was going at a hand gallop. Right before the door he reined in his horse with a sudden jerk, so that he made a deep gash in the sand; and swinging his sword, he shouted, "They're coming, they're coming!"

"Who are coming?" asked Rebecca.

"Snorting black chargers and three war chariots full of men-at-arms."

"Rubbish, my boy!" said his father, sternly.

"Three phaetons are coming with townspeople in them," said Ansgarius, and dismounted with an abashed air.

"Let us go in, Rebecca," said the Pastor, turning.

But at the same moment the foremost horses came at a quick pace over the brow of the hill. They were not exactly snorting chargers; yet it was a pretty sight as carriage after carriage came into view in the sunshine, full of merry faces and lively colors. Rebecca could not help stopping.

On the back seat of the foremost carriage sat an elderly gentleman and a buxom lady. On the front seat she saw a young lady; and just as they entered the yard, a gentleman who sat at her side stood up, and, with a word of apology to the lady on the back seat, turned and looked forward past the driver. Rebecca gazed at him without knowing what she was doing.

"How lovely it is here!" cried the young man.

For the Parsonage lay on the outermost slope towards the sea, so that the vast blue horizon suddenly burst upon you as you entered the yard.

The gentleman on the back seat leaned a little forward. " Yes, it's very pretty here," he said; " I'm glad that you appreciate our peculiar scenery, Mr. Lintzow."

At the same moment the young man's glance met Rebecca's, and she instantly lowered her eyes. But he stopped the driver, and cried, "Let us remain here !"

"Hush !" said the older lady, with a low laugh. "This won't do, Mr. Lintzow: this is the Parsonage."

" It doesn't matter," cried the young man, merrily, as he jumped out of the carriage. "I say," he shouted backward towards the other carriages, "sha'n't we rest here ?"

" Yes, yes," came the answer in chorus ; and the merry party began at once to alight.

But now the gentleman on the back seat rose, and said, seriously : " No, no, my friends ! this really won't do ! It's out of the question for us to descend upon the clergyman, whom we don't know at all. It's only ten minutes' drive to the district judge's, and there they are in the habit of receiving strangers."

He was on the point of giving orders to drive on, when the Pastor appeared in the door-way, with a friendly bow. He knew Consul Hartvig by sight —the leading man of the town.

" If your party will make the best of things here, it will be a great pleasure to me ; and I think I may say that, so far as the view goes —"

"Oh no, my dear Pastor, you're altogether too
kind ; it's out of the question for us to accept your
kind invitation, and I must really beg you to excuse
these young madcaps," said Mrs. Hartvig, half in
despair when she saw her youngest son, who had
been seated in the last carriage, already deep in a
confidential chat with Ansgarius.

" But I assure you, Mrs. Hartvig," answered the
Pastor, smiling, " that so pleasant an interruption
of our solitude would be most welcome both to my
daughter and myself."

Mr. Lintzow opened the carriage - door with a
formal bow, Consul Hartvig looked at his wife and
she at him, the Pastor advanced and renewed his
invitation, and the end was that, with half-laughing
reluctance, they alighted and suffered the Pastor
to usher them into the spacious garden-room.

Then came renewed excuses and introductions.
The party consisted of Consul Hartvig's children
and some young friends of theirs, the picnic having been arranged in honor of Max Lintzow, a friend
of the eldest son of the house, who was spending
some days as the Consul's guest.

" My daughter Rebecca," said the Pastor, pre-
senting her, " who will do the best our humble
house-keeping permits."

" No, no, I protest, my dear Pastor," the lively
Mrs. Hartvig interrupted him eagerly, " this is going too far ! Even if this incorrigible Mr. Lintzow
and my crazy sons have succeeded in storming

your house and home, I won't resign the last rem-
nants of my authority. The entertainment shall
most certainly be my affair. Off you go, young
men," she said, turning to her sons, "and unpack
the carriages. And you, my dear child, must by all
means go and amuse yourself with the young people ; just leave the catering to me ; I know all about
that."

And the kind-hearted woman looked with her
honest gray eyes at her host's pretty daughter, and
patted her on the cheek.

How nice that felt ! There was a peculiar cozi-
ness in the touch of the comfortable old lady's soft
hand. The tears almost rose to Rebecca's eyes;
she stood as if she expected that the strange lady
would put her arms round her neck and whisper to
her something she had long waited to hear.

But the conversation glided on. The young people, with ever-increasing glee, brought all sorts of
strange parcels out of the carriages. Mrs. Hartvig
threw her cloak upon a chair and set about arrang-
ing things as best she could. But the young people,
always with Mr. Lintzow at their head, seemed determined to make as much confusion as possible.
Even the Pastor was infected by their merriment,
and to Rebecca's unspeakable astonishment she
saw her own father, in complicity with Mr. Lintzow, hiding a big paper parcel under Mrs. Hartvig's cloak.

At last the racket became too much for the old

lady. "My dear Miss Rebecca," she exclaimed,
"have you not any show-place to exhibit in the
neighborhood—the farther off the better—so that
I might get these crazy beings off my hands for a
little while?"

"There's a lovely view from the King's Knoll;
and then there's the beach and the sea."

"Yes, let's go down to the sea!" cried Max Lintzow.

"That's just what I want," said the old lady.
"If you can relieve me of *him* I shall be all right,
for he is the worst of them all."

"If Miss Rebecca will lead the way, I will follow wherever she pleases," said the young man,
with a bow.

Rebecca blushed. Nothing of that sort had ever
been said to her before. The handsome young
man made her a low bow, and his words had such
a ring of sincerity. But there was no time to dwell
upon this impression; the whole merry troop were
soon out of the house, through the garden, and, with
Rebecca and Lintzow at their head, making their
way up to the little height which was called the
King's Knoll.

Many years ago a number of antiquities had
been dug up on the top of the Knoll, and one of
the Pastor's predecessors in the parish had planted
some hardy trees upon the slopes. With the ex-
ception of a rowan-tree, and a walnut-avenue in the
Parsonage garden, these were the only trees to be

found for miles round on the windy slopes facing
the open sea.   In spite of storms and sand-drifts,
they had, in the course of time, reached something
like the height of a man, and, turning their bare
and gnarled stems to the north wind, like a bent
back, they stretched forth their long, yearning arms
towards the south.   Rebecca's mother had planted
some violets among them.

"Oh, how fortunate!" cried the eldest Miss Hartvig; "here are violets!   Oh, Mr. Lintzow, do pick
me a bouquet of them for this evening!"

The young man, who had been exerting himself
to hit upon the right tone in which to converse
with Rebecca, fancied that the girl started at Miss
Frederica's words.

"You are very fond of the violets?" he said, softly.

She looked up at him in surprise; how could he
possibly know that?

"Don't you think, Miss Hartvig, that it would be
better to pick the flowers just as we are starting, so
that they may keep fresher?"

"As you please," she answered, shortly.

"Let's hope she'll forget all about it by that time,"
said Max Lintzow to himself, under his breath.

But Rebecca heard, and wondered what pleasure he could find in protecting her violets, instead
of picking them for that handsome girl.

After they had spent some time in admiring the
limitless prospect, the party left the Knoll and took
a foot-path downward towards the beach.

On the smooth, firm sand, at the very verge of the sea, the young people strolled along, conversing gayly. Rebecca was at first quite confused. It seemed as though these merry towns-people spoke a language she did not understand. Sometimes she thought they laughed at nothing; and, on the other hand, she herself often could not help laughing at their cries of astonishment and their questions about everything they saw.

But gradually she began to feel at her ease among these good-natured, kindly people; the youngest Miss Hartvig even put her arm around her waist as they walked. And then Rebecca, too, thawed; she joined in their laughter, and said what she had to say as easily and freely as any of the others. It never occurred to her to notice that the young men, and especially Mr. Lintzow, were chiefly taken up with her; and the little pointed speeches which this circumstance called forth from time to time were as meaningless for her as much of the rest of the conversation.

They amused themselves for some time with running down the shelving beach every time the wave receded, and then rushing up again when the next wave came. And great was the glee when one of the young men was overtaken, or when a larger wave than usual sent its fringe of foam right over the slope, and forced the merry party to beat a precipitate retreat.

"Look! Mamma's afraid that we shall be too

late for the ball," cried Miss Hartvig, suddenly;
and they now discovered that the Consul and Mrs.
Hartvig and the Pastor were standing like three
windmills on the Parsonage hill, waving with pocket-
handkerchiefs and napkins.

They turned their faces homeward. Rebecca
took them by a short cut over the morass, not re-
flecting that the ladies from the town could not
jump from tuft to tuft as she could. Miss Frederica, in her tight skirt, jumped short, and stumbled
into a muddy hole. She shrieked and cried pit-
eously for help, with her eyes fixed upon Lintzow.

"Look alive, Henrik!" cried Max to Hartvig jun-
ior, who was nearer at hand; "why don't you help
your sister?"

Miss Frederica extricated herself without help,
and the party proceeded.

The table was laid in the garden, along the wall
of the house; and although the spring was so young,
it was warm enough in the sunshine. When they
had all found seats, Mrs. Hartvig cast a searching
glance over the table.

"Why—why—surely there's something wanting!
I'm convinced I saw the house-keeper wrapping
up a black grouse this morning. Frederica, my
dear, don't you remember it?"

"Excuse me, mother, you know that house-keeping is not at all in my department."

Rebecca looked at her father, and so did Lintzow; the worthy Pastor pulled a face upon which even Ansgarius could read a confession of crime.

"I can't possibly believe," began Mrs. Hartvig, "that you, Pastor, have been conspiring with—" And then he could not help laughing and making a clean breast of it, amid great merriment, while the boys in triumph produced the parcel with the game. Every one was in the best possible humor. Consul Hartvig was delighted to find that their clerical host could join in a joke, and the Pastor himself was in higher spirits than he had been in for many a year.

In the course of the conversation some one happened to remark that although the arrangements might be countrified enough, the viands were too town-like; "No country meal is complete without thick milk."*

Rebecca at once rose and demanded leave to bring a basin of milk; and, paying no attention to Mrs. Hartvig's protests, she left the table.

"Let me help you, Miss Rebecca," cried Max, and ran after her.

"That is a lively young man," said the Pastor.

"Yes, isn't he?" answered the Consul, "and a deuced good business man into the bargain. He has spent several years abroad, and now his father has taken him into partnership."

---

* Milk allowed to stand until it has thickened to the consistency of curds, and then eaten, commonly with sugar.

3

"He's perhaps a little unstable," said Mrs. Hart-vig, doubtfully.

"Yes, he is indeed," sighed Miss Frederica.

The young man followed Rebecca through the suite of rooms that led to the dairy. At bottom, she did not like this, although the dairy was her pride; but he joked and laughed so merrily that she could not help joining in the laughter.

She chose a basin of milk upon the upper shelf, and stretched out her arms to reach it.

"No, no, Miss Rebecca, it's too high for you!" cried Max; "let me hand it down to you." And as he said so he laid his hand upon hers.

Rebecca hastily drew back her hand. She knew that her face had flushed, and she almost felt as if she must burst into tears.

Then he said, softly and earnestly, lowering his eyes, "Pray, pardon me, Miss Rebecca. I feel that my behavior must seem far too light and frivolous to such a woman as you; but I should be sorry that you should think of me as nothing but the empty coxcomb I appear to be. Merriment, to many people, is merely a cloak for their sufferings, and there are some who laugh only that they may not weep."

At the last words he looked up. There was something so mournful, and at the same time so reverential, in his glance, that Rebecca all of a sudden felt as if she had been unkind to him. She was accustomed to reach things down from the up-

per shelf, but when she again stretched out her
hands for the basin of milk, she let her arms drop,
and said, " No, perhaps it *is* too high for me, after
all."

A faint smile passed over his face as he took
the basin and carried it carefully out; she accompanied him and opened the doors for him. Every
time he passed her she looked closely at him. His
collar, his necktie, his coat—everything was different from her father's, and he carried with him a
peculiar perfume which she did not know.

When they came to the garden door, he stopped
for an instant, and looked up with a melancholy
smile : " I must take a moment to recover my ex
pression of gayety, so that no one out there may
notice anything."

Then he passed out upon the steps with a joking
speech to the company at the table, and she heard
their laughing answers; but she herself remained
behind in the garden-room.

Poor young man ! how sorry she was for him;
and how strange that she of all people should be
the only one in whom he confided. What secret
sorrow could it be that depressed him ? Perhaps
he, too, had lost his mother. Or could it be something still more terrible ? How glad she would be
if only she could help him.

When Rebecca presently came out he was once
more the blithest of them all. Only once in a while,
when he looked at her, his eyes seemed again to

assume that melancholy, half-beseeching expression ; and it cut her to the heart when he laughed at the same moment.

At last came the time for departure ; there was hearty leave-taking on both sides. But as the last of the packing was going on, and in the general confusion, while every one was finding his place in the carriages, or seeking a new place for the homeward journey, Rebecca slipped into the house, through the rooms, out into the garden, and away to the King's Knoll. Here she seated herself in the shadow of the trees, where the violets grew, and tried to collect her thoughts.

—"What about the violets, Mr. Lintzow?" cried Miss Frederica, who had already taken her seat in the carriage.

The young man had for some time been eagerly searching for the daughter of the house. He answered absently, " I'm afraid it's too late."

But a thought seemed suddenly to strike him. "Oh, Mrs. Hartvig," he cried, " will you excuse me for a couple of minutes while I fetch a bouquet for Miss Frederica?"

—Rebecca heard rapid steps approaching ; she thought it could be no one but he.

" Ah, are you here, Miss Rebecca ? I have come to gather some violets."

She turned half away from him and began to pluck the flowers.

" Are these flowers for me?" he asked, hesitatingly.

" Are they not for Miss Frederica ?"

" Oh no, let them be for me !" he besought, kneel-
ing at her side.

Again his voice had such a plaintive ring in it—
almost like that of a begging child.

She handed him the violets without looking up.
Then he clasped her round the waist and held her
close to him. She did not resist, but closed her
eyes and breathed heavily. Then she felt that he
kissed her—over and over again—on the eyes, on
the mouth, meanwhile calling her by her name,
with incoherent words, and then kissing her again.
They called to him from the garden ; he let her go
and ran down the mound. The horses stamped,
the young man sprang quickly into the carriage,
and it rolled away. But as he was closing the
carriage door he was so maladroit as to drop
the bouquet; only a single violet remained in his
hand.

" I suppose it's no use offering you this *one*, Miss
Frederica?" he said.

" No. thanks : you may keep that as a memento
of your remarkable dexterity," answered Miss Hartvig ; he was in her black books.

" Yes—you are right—I shall do so," answered
Max Lintzow, with perfect composure.

—Next day, after the ball, when he put on his
morning-coat, he found a withered violet in the
button-hole. He nipped off the flower with his fingers, and drew out the stalk from beneath.

"By-the-bye," he said, smiling to himself in the mirror, "I had almost forgotten *her!*"

In the afternoon he went away, and then he *quite* forgot her.

The summer came with warm days and long, luminous nights. The smoke of the passing steamships lay in long black streaks over the peaceful sea. The sailing-ships drifted by with flapping sails and took nearly a whole day to pass out of sight.

It was some time before the Pastor noticed any change in his daughter. But little by little he became aware that Rebecca was not flourishing that summer. She had grown pale, and kept much to her own room. She scarcely ever came into the study, and at last he fancied that she avoided him.

Then he spoke seriously to her, and begged her to tell him if she was ill, or if mental troubles of any sort had affected her spirits.

But she only wept, and answered scarcely a word.

After this conversation, however, things went rather better. She did not keep so much by herself, and was oftener with her father. But the old ring was gone from her voice, and her eyes were not so frank as of old.

The Doctor came, and began to cross-question her. She blushed as red as fire, and at last burst into such a paroxysm of weeping, that the old gentleman left her room and went down to the Pastor in his study.

"Well, Doctor, what do you think of Rebecca?"

"Tell me now, Pastor," began the Doctor, diplomatically, "has your daughter gone through any violent mental crisis—hm—any—"

"Temptation, do you mean?"

"No, not exactly. Has she not had any sort of heartache? Or, to put it plainly, any love-sorrow?"

The Pastor was very near feeling a little hurt. How could the Doctor suppose that his own Rebecca, whose heart was as an open book to him, could or would conceal from her father any sorrow of such a nature! And, besides—! Rebecca was really not one of the girls whose heads were full of romantic dreams of love. And as she was never away from his side, how could she—? "No, no, my dear Doctor! That diagnosis does you little credit!" the Pastor concluded, with a tranquil smile.

"Well, well, there's no harm done!" said the old Doctor, and wrote a prescription which was at least innocuous. He knew of no simples to cure love-sorrows; but in his heart of hearts he held to his diagnosis.

The visit of the Doctor had frightened Rebecca. She now kept still stricter watch upon herself, and redoubled her exertions to seem as before. For no one must suspect what had happened: that a young man, an utter stranger, had held her in his arms and kissed her over and over again!

As often as she realized this the blood rushed

to her cheeks. She washed herself ten times in the day, yet it seemed she could never be clean.

For what was it that had happened? Was it not the last extremity of shame? Was she now any better than the many wretched girls whose errors she had shuddered to think of, and had never been able to understand? Ah, if there were only any one she could question! If she could only unburden her mind of all the doubt and uncertainty that tortured her; learn clearly what she had done; find out if she had still the right to look her father in the face—or if she were the most miserable of all sinners.

Her father often asked her if she could not confide to him what was weighing on her mind: for he felt that she was keeping something from him. But when she looked into his clear eyes, into his pure open face, it seemed impossible, literally impossible, to approach that terrible impure point—and she only wept. She thought sometimes of that good Mrs. Hartvig's soft hand; but she was a stranger, and far away. So she must e'en fight out her fight in utter solitude, and so quietly that no one should be aware of it.

And he, who was pursuing his path through life with so bright a countenance and so heavy a heart! Should she ever see him again? And if she were ever to meet him, where should she hide herself? He was an inseparable part of all her doubt and pain; but she felt no bitterness, no resentment towards him. All that she suffered bound her closer to him, and he was never out of her thoughts.

In the daily duties of the household Rebecca was as punctual and careful as ever. But in everything she did he was present to her memory. Innumerable spots in the house and garden recalled him to her thoughts; she met him in the door-ways; she remembered where he stood when first he spoke to her. She had never been at the King's Knoll since that day; it was there that he had clasped her round the waist, and—kissed her.

The Pastor was full of solicitude about his daughter; but whenever the Doctor's hint occurred to him he shook his head, half angrily. How could he dream that a practised hand, with a well-worn trick of the fence, could pierce the armor of proof with which he had provided her?

If the spring had been late, the autumn was early.

One fine warm summer evening it suddenly began to rain. The next day it was still raining; and it poured incessantly, growing ever colder and colder, for eleven days and nights on end. At last it cleared up, but the next night there were four degrees of frost.*

On the bushes and trees the leaves hung glued together after the long rain; and when the frost

* Réaumur.

had dried them after its fashion, they fell to the
ground in multitudes at every little puff of wind.

The Pastor's tenant was one of the few that had
got their corn in; and now it had to be threshed
while there was water for the machine. The little
brook in the valley rushed foaming along, as brown
as coffee, and all the men on the farm were taken
up with tending the machine and carting corn and
straw up and down the Parsonage hill.

The farm-yard was bestrewn with straw, and
when the wind swirled in between the houses it
seized the oat-straws by the head, raised them on
end, and set them dancing along like yellow spec-
tres. It was the juvenile autumn wind trying its
strength; not until well on in the winter, when it
has full-grown lungs, does it take to playing with
tiles and chimney-pots.

A sparrow sat crouched together upon the dog-
kennel; it drew its head down among its feathers,
blinked its eyes, and betrayed no interest in anything. But in reality it noted carefully where the
corn was deposited. In the great sparrow-battle
of the spring it had been in the very centre of the
ball, and had pecked and screamed with the best
of them. But it had sobered down since then; it
thought of its wife and children, and reflected how
good it was to have something in reserve against
the winter

—Ansgarius looked forward to the winter—to perilous expeditions through the snow-drifts and pitch

dark evenings with thundering breakers. He already turned to account the ice which lay on the puddles after the frosty nights, by making all his tin soldiers, with two brass cannons, march out upon it. Stationed upon an overturned bucket, he watched the ice giving way, little by little, until the whole army was immersed, and only the wheels of the cannons remained visible. Then he shouted, "Hurrah!" and swung his cap.

"What are you shouting about?" asked the Pastor, who happened to pass through the farm-yard.

"I'm playing at Austerlitz!" answered Ansgarius, beaming.

The father passed on, sighing mournfully; he could not understand his children

—Down in the garden sat Rebecca on a bench in the sun. She looked out over the heather, which was in purple flower, while the meadows were putting on their autumn pallor.

The lapwings were gathering in silence, and holding flying-drills in preparation for their journey; and all the strand-birds were assembling, in order to take flight together. Even the lark had lost its courage and was seeking convoy—voiceless and unknown among the other gray autumn birds. But the sea-gull stalked peaceably about, protruding its crop; it was not under notice to quit.

The air was so still and languid and hazy. All sounds and colors were toning down against the winter, and that was very pleasant to her.

She was weary, and the long dead winter would suit her well. She knew that her winter would be longer than all the others, and she began to shrink from the spring.

Then everything would awaken that the winter had laid to sleep. The birds would come back and sing the old songs with new voices; and upon the King's Knoll her mother's violets would peer forth afresh in azure clusters; it was there that he had clasped her round the waist and kissed her—over and over again.

THE PEAT MOOR.

THE PEAT MOOR.

HIGH over the heathery wastes flew a wise old raven.

He was bound many miles westward, right out to the sea-coast, to unearth a sow's ear which he had buried in the good times.

It was now late autumn, and food was scarce.

When you see one raven, says Father Brehm, you need only look round to discover a second.

But you might have looked long enough where this wise old raven came flying; he was, and remained, alone. And without troubling about anything or uttering a sound, he sped on his strong coal-black wings through the dense rain-mist, steering due west.

But as he flew, evenly and meditatively, his sharp eyes searched the landscape beneath, and the old bird was full of chagrin.

Year by year the little green and yellow patches down there increased in number and size; rood after rood was cut out of the heathery waste, little houses sprang up with red-tiled roofs and low chimneys breathing oily peat-reek. Men and their meddling everywhere!

He remembered how, in the days of his youth—several winters ago, of course—this was the very place for a wide-awake raven with a family: long, interminable stretches of heather, swarms of leverets and little birds, eider-ducks on the shore with delicious big eggs, and tidbits of all sorts abundant as heart could desire.

Now he saw house upon house, patches of yellow corn-land and green meadows; and food was so scarce that a gentlemanly old raven had to fly miles and miles for a paltry sow's ear.

Oh, those men! those men! The old bird knew them.

He had grown up among men, and, what was more, among the aristocracy. He had passed his childhood and youth at the great house close to the town.

But now, whenever he passed over the house, he soared high into the air, so as not to be recognized. For when he saw a female figure down in the garden, he thought it was the young lady of the house, wearing powdered hair and a white head-dress; whereas it was in reality her daughter, with snow-white curls and a widow's cap.

Had he enjoyed his life among the aristocracy? Oh, that's as you please to look at it. There was plenty to eat and plenty to learn; but, after all, it was captivity. During the first years his left wing was clipped, and afterwards, as his old master used to say, he was upon *parole d'honneur*.

This parole he had broken one spring when a glossy-black young she-raven happened to fly over the garden.

Some time afterwards—a few winters had slipped away — he came back to the house. But some strange boys threw stones at him ; the old master and the young lady were not at home.

" No doubt they are in town," thought the old raven ; and he came again some time later. But he met with just the same reception.

Then the gentlemenly old bird—for in the meantime he had grown old—felt hurt, and now he flew high over the house. He would have nothing more to do with men, and the old master and the young lady might look for him as long as they pleased. That they did so he never doubted.

And he forgot all that he had learned, both the difficult French words which the young lady taught him in the drawing-room, and the incomparably easier expletives which he had picked up on his own account in the servants' hall.

Only two human sounds clung to his memory, the last relics of his vanished learning. When he was in a thoroughly good-humor, he would often say. " Bonjour, madame !" But when he was angry, he shrieked. " Go to the devil !"

Through the dense rain-mist he sped swiftly and unswervingly ; already he saw the white wreath of

4

surf along the coast. Then he descried a great
black waste stretching out beneath him. It was a
peat moor.

It was encircled with farms on the heights around;
but on the low plain—it must have been over a mile*
long—there was no trace of human meddling; only
a few stacks of peat on the outskirts, with black
hummocks and gleaming water-holes between them.

" Bonjour, madame!" cried the old raven, and
began to wheel in great circles over the moor. It
looked so inviting that he settled downward, slowly and warily, and alighted upon a tree-root in the
midst of it.

Here it was just as in the old days —a silent
wilderness. On some scattered patches of drier
soil there grew a little short heather and a few
clumps of rushes. They were withered; but on
their stiff stems there still hung one or two tufts —
black, and sodden by the autumn rain. For the
most part the soil was fine, black, and crumbling—
wet and full of water-holes. Gray and twisted
tree-roots stuck up above the surface, interlaced
like a gnarled net-work.

The old raven well understood all that he saw.
There had been trees here in the old times, before
even his day.

The wood had disappeared; branches, leaves,
everything was gone. Only the tangled roots re-

---

* One Norwegian mile is equal to seven English miles.

mained, deep down in the soft mass of black fibres
and water.

But further than this, change could not possibly
go ; so it must endure, and here, at any rate, men
would have to stint their meddling.

The old bird held himself erect. The farms lay
so far away that he felt securely at home, here in
the middle of the bottomless morass. One relic, at
least, of antiquity must remain undisturbed. He
smoothed his glossy black feathers, and said several times, " Bonjour, madame !"

But down from the nearest farm came a couple
of men with a horse and cart ; two small boys ran
behind. They took a crooked course among the
hummocks, but made as though to cross the morass.

" They must soon stop," thought the raven.

But they drew nearer and nearer ; the old bird
turned his head uneasily from side to side ; it was
strange that they should venture so far out.

At last they stopped, and the men set to work
with spades and axes. The raven could see that
they were struggling with a huge root which they
wanted to loosen.

" They will soon tire of that," thought the raven.

But they did not tire , they hacked with their
axes—the sharpest the raven had ever seen—they
dug and hauled, and at last they actually got the
huge stem turned over on its side, so that the whole
tough net-work of roots stood straight up in the
air.

The small boys wearied of digging canals between the water-holes. "Look at that great big crow over there," said one of them.

They armed themselves with a stone in each hand, and came sneaking forward behind the hummocks.

The raven saw them quite well. But that was not the worst thing it saw.

Not even out on the morass was antiquity to be left in peace. He had now seen that even the gray tree-roots, older than the oldest raven, and firmly inwoven into the deep, bottomless morass— that even they had to yield before the sharp axes.

And when the boys had got so near that they were on the point of opening fire, he raised his heavy wings and soared aloft.

But as he rose into the air and looked down upon the toiling men and the stupid boys, who stood gaping at him with a stone in each hand, a great wrath seized the old bird.

He swooped down upon the boys like an eagle, and while his great wings flounced about their ears, he shrieked in a terrible voice, " Go to the devil !"

The boys gave a yell and threw themselves down upon the ground. When they presently ventured to look up again, all was still and deserted as before. Far away, a solitary black bird winged to the westward.

But till they grew to be men—aye, even to their

dying day — they were firmly convinced that the Evil One himself had appeared to them out on the black morass, in the form of a monstrous black bird with eyes of fire.

But it was only an old raven, flying westward to unearth a sow's ear which it had buried.

"HOPE'S CLAD IN APRIL GREEN."

"YOU'RE kicking up the dust!" cried Cousin Hans.

Ola did not hear.

"He's quite as deaf as Aunt Maren," thought Hans. "You're kicking up the dust!" he shouted, louder.

"Oh, I beg your pardon!" said Cousin Ola, and lifted his feet high in air at every step. Not for all the world would he do anything to annoy his brother; he had too much on his conscience already.

Was he not at this very moment thinking of her whom he knew that his brother loved? And was it not sinful of him to be unable to conquer a passion which, besides being a wrong towards his own brother, was so utterly hopeless?

Cousin Ola took himself sternly to task, and while he kept to the other side of the way, so as not to make a dust, he tried with all his might to think of the most indifferent things. But however far away his thoughts might start, they always returned by the strangest short-cuts to the forbidden point, and began once more to flutter around it, like moths around a candle.

The brothers, who were paying a holiday visit to their uncle, the Pastor, were now on their way to the Sheriff's house, where there was to be a dancing-party for young people. There were many students paying visits in the neighborhood, so that these parties passed like an epidemic from house to house.

Cousin Hans was thus in his very element; he sang, he danced, he was entertaining from morning to night; and if his tone had been a little sharp when he declared that Ola was kicking up the dust, it was really because of his annoyance at being unable, by any means, to screw his brother up to the same pitch of hilarity.

We already know what was oppressing Ola. But even under ordinary circumstances he was more quiet and retiring than his brother. He danced "like a pair of nut-crackers," said Hans; he could not sing at all (Cousin Hans even declared that his speaking voice was monotonous and unsympathetic); and, in addition to all this, he was rather absent and ill-at-ease in the society of ladies.

As they approached the Sheriff's house, they heard a carriage behind them.

"That's the Doctor's people," said Hans, placing himself in position for bowing; for the beloved one was the daughter of the district physician.

"Oh, how lovely she is — in light pink!" said Cousin Hans.

Cousin Ola saw at once that the beloved one was in light green; but he dared not say a word lest he should betray himself by his voice, for his heart was in his throat.

The carriage passed at full speed; the young men bowed, and the old Doctor cried out, "Come along!"

"Why, I declare, that was she in light green!" said Cousin Hans; he had barely had time to transfer his burning glance from the light-pink frock to the light-green. "But wasn't she lovely, Ola?"

"Oh yes," answered Ola with an effort.

"What a cross-grained being you are!" exclaimed Hans, indignantly. "But even if you're devoid of all sense for female beauty, I think you might at least show more interest in — in your brother's future wife."

" If you only knew how she interests me," thought the nefarious Ola, hanging his head.

But meanwhile this delightful meeting had thrown Hans into an ecstatic mood of amorous bliss, he swung his stick, snapped his fingers, and sang at the pitch of his voice.

As he thought of the fair one in the light-green frock—fresh as spring, airy as a butterfly, he called it—the refrain of an old ditty rose to his lips, and he sang it with great enjoyment:

"Hope's clad in April green—
    Trommelommelom, trommelommelom,
    Tender it's vernal sheen—
    Trommelommelom, trommelommelom."

This verse seemed to him eminently suited to the situation, and he repeated it over and over again— now in the waltz-time of the old melody, now as a march, and again as a serenade—now in loud, jubilant tones, and then half whispering, as if he were confiding his love and his hope to the moon and the silent groves.

Cousin Ola was almost sick ; for, great as was his respect for his brother's singing, he became at last so dog-tired of this April-green hope and this eternal "Trommelommelom" that it was a great relief to him when they at last arrived at the Sheriff's.

The afternoon passed as it always does on such occasions, they all enjoyed themselves mightily. For most of them were in love, and those who were not found almost a greater pleasure in keeping an eye upon those who were.

Some one proposed a game of "La Grace" in the garden. Cousin Hans rushed nimbly about and played a thousand pranks, threw the game into confusion, and paid his partner all sorts of attentions.

Cousin Ola stood at his post and gave his whole mind to his task ; he caught the ring and sent it off again with never-failing precision. Ola would have enjoyed himself, too, if only his conscience had not so bitterly upbraided him for his nefarious love for his brother's "future wife."

When the evening began to grow cool the party went in-doors, and the dancing began.

Ola did not dance much at any time, but to-day he was not at all in the humor. He occupied himself in observing Hans, who spent the whole evening in worshipping his lady-love. A spasm shot through Ola's heart when he saw the light-green frock whirl away in his brother's arms, and it seemed to him that they danced every dance together.

At last came the time for breaking up. Most of the older folks had already taken their departure in their respective carriages, the young people having resolved to see each other home in the delicious moonlight.

But when the last galop was over, the hostess would not hear of the young ladies going right out into the evening air, while they were still warm with dancing. She therefore decreed half an hour for cooling down, and, to occupy this time in the pleasantest manner, she begged Cousin Hans to sing a little song.

He was ready at once, he was not one of those foolish people who require pressing; he knew quite well the value of his talent.

There was, however, this peculiarity about Hans's singing, or rather about its reception, that opinion was more than usually divided as to its merits. By three persons in the world his execution was admired as something incomparable. These three persons were, first, Cousin Ola, then Aunt Maren, and lastly Cousin Hans himself. Then there was a large party which thought it great fun to hear Cousin Hans sing. "He always makes something out of it." But lastly there came a few evil-disposed people who asserted that he could neither sing nor play.

It was with respect to the latter point, the accompaniment, that Cousin Ola always cherished a secret reproach against his brother—the only shadow upon his admiration for him.

He knew how much labor it had cost both Hans himself and his sisters to get him drilled in these accompaniments, especially in the three minor chords with which he always finished up, and which he practised beforehand every time he went to a party.

So, when he saw his brother seated at the piano, letting his fingers run lightly and carelessly over the key-board, and then looking up to the ceiling and muttering, "What key is it in again?" as if he were searching for the right one, a shiver always ran through Cousin Ola. For he knew that Hans had mastered three accompaniments, and no more —one minor and two major.

And when the singer, before rising from the piano, threw in these three carefully-practised minor chords so lightly, and with such an impromptu

air, as if his fingers had instinctively chanced upon
them, then Ola shook his head and said to himself,
" This is not quite straightforward of Hans."

In the mean time his brother sang away at his rich
repertory. Schumann and Kierulf were his favor-
ites, so he performed "*Du bist die Ruh,*" "*My loved
one, I am prison'd,*" "*Ich grolle nicht,*" "*Die alten bösen
Lieder,*" "*I lay my all, love, at thy feet,*" "*Aus meinen
grossen Schmerzen mach' ich die kleinen Lieder*"—all
with the same calm superiority, and that light, half-
sportive accompaniment. The only thing that gave
him a little trouble was that ·fatal point, "*Ich legt'
auch meine Liebe, Und meinen Schmerz hinein;*" but
even of this he made something.

Then Ola, who knew to a nicety the limits of his
brother's musical accomplishment, noticed that he
was leaving the beaten track, and beginning to
wander among the keys; and presently he was
horrified to find that Hans was groping after that
unhappy " Hope's clad in April green." But fortunately he could not hit upon it, so he confined
himself to humming the song half aloud, while he
threw in the three famous minor chords.

" Now we're quite cool again," cried the fair one
in light green, hastily.

There was a general burst of laughter at her
eagerness to get away, and she was quite crimson
when she said good-night.

Cousin Ola, who was standing near the hostess,
also took his leave. Cousin Hans, on the other

hand, was detained by the Sheriff, who was anxious to learn under what teachers he had studied music; and that took time.

Thus it happened that Ola and the fair one in the light green passed out into the passage at the same time. There the young folks were crowding round the hat-pegs, some to find their own wraps, some to take down other people's.

"I suppose it's no good trying to push our way forward," said the fair one.

Ola's windpipe contracted in such a vexatious way that he only succeeded in uttering a meaningless sound. They stood close to each other in the crush, and Ola would gladly have given a finger to be able to say something pleasant to her, or at least something rational; but he found it quite impossible.

"Of course you've enjoyed the evening?" said she, in a friendly tone.

Cousin Ola thought of the pitiful part he had been playing all evening; his unsociableness weighed so much upon his mind that he answered—the very stupidest thing he could have answered, he thought, the moment the words were out of his lips—"I'm so sorry that I can't sing."

"I suppose it's a family failing," answered the fair one, with a rapid glance.

"N—n—no," said Ola, exceedingly put out, "my brother sings capitally."

"Do you think so?" she said, drily.

This was the most astounding thing that had ever
happened to Ola : that there could be more than
one opinion about his brother's singing, and that
she, his "future wife," did not seem to admire it !
And yet it was not quite unpleasant to him to hear it.

Again there was a silence, which Ola sought in
vain to break.

" Don't you care for dancing ?" she asked.

" Not with every one," he blurted out.

She laughed : " No, no ; but gentlemen have the
right to choose."

Now Ola began to lose his footing. He felt like
a man who is walking, lost in thought, through
the streets on a winter evening, and who suddenly
discovers that he has got upon a patch of slippery
ice. There was nothing for it but to keep up and
go ahead ; so, with the courage of despair, he said :
" If I knew—or dared to hope — that one of the
ladies — no — that the lady I wanted to dance with —
that she would care to—him—that she would dance
with me, then—then—" he could get no further,
and after saying " then " two or three times over,
he came to a stand-still.

" You could ask her," said the fair one.

Her bracelet had come unfastened, and its clasp
was so stiff that she had to bend right forward and
pinch it so hard that she became quite red in the
face, in order to fasten it again.

" Would you, for example, dance with me ?"
Ola's brain was swimming.

5

"Why not?" she answered. She stood pressing the point of her shoe into a crack in the floor.

"We're to have a party at the Parsonage on Friday—would you give me a dance then?"

"With pleasure: which would you like?" she answered, trying her best to assume a "society" manner.

"A quadrille?" said Ola; thinking: "Quadrilles are so long."

"The second quadrille is disengaged," answered the lady.

"And a galop?"

"Yes, thank you; the first galop," she replied, with a little hesitation.

"And a polka?"

"No, no! no more," cried the fair one, looking at Ola with alarm.

At the same moment, Hans came rushing along at full speed. "Oh, how lucky I am to find you!— but in what company!"

Thereupon he took possession of the fair one in his amiable fashion, and drew her away with him to find her wraps and join the others.

"A quadrille and a galop: but no more—so so! so so!" repeated Cousin Ola. He stood as though rooted to the spot. At last he became aware that he was alone. He hastily seized a hat, slunk out by the back way, sneaked through the garden, and clambered with great difficulty over the garden fence, not far from the gate which stood ajar.

He struck into the first foot-path through the fields, fixing his eyes upon the Parsonage chimneys. He was vaguely conscious that he was getting wet up to the knees in the long grass; but on the other hand, he was not in the least aware that the Sheriff's old uniform cap, which he had had the luck to snatch up in his haste, was waggling about upon his head, until at last it came to rest when the long peak slipped down over his ear.

"A quadrille and a galop; but no more—so so ! so so !—"

—It was pretty well on in the night when Hans approached the Parsonage. He had seen the ladies of the Doctor's party home, and was now making up the accounts of the day as he went along.

"She's a little shy; but on the whole I don't dislike that."

When he left the road at the Parsonage garden, he said, "She's dreadfully shy—almost more than I care for."

But as he crossed the farm-yard, he vowed that coy and capricious girls were the most intolerable creatures he knew. The thing was that he did not feel at all satisfied with the upshot of the day. Not that he for a moment doubted that she loved him; but, just on that account, he thought her coldness and reserve doubly annoying. She had never once thrown the ring to him; she had never once singled him out in the cotillion; and on the way home she had talked to every one but him. But he would

adopt a different policy the next time; she should
soon come to repent that day.

He slipped quietly into the house, so that his
uncle might not hear how late he was. In order to
reach his own and his brother's bedroom he had to
pass through a long attic. A window in this attic
was used by the young men as a door through which
to reach a sort of balcony, formed by the canopy
over the steps leading into the garden.

Cousin Hans noticed that this window was standing open; and out upon the balcony, in the clear
moonlight, he saw his brother's figure.

Ola still wore his white dancing-gloves; he held
on to the railing with both hands, and stared the
moon straight in the face.

Cousin Hans could not understand what his
brother was doing out there at that time of night,
and least of all could he understand what had in-
duced him to put a flower-pot on his head.

"He must be drunk," thought Hans, approaching
him warily.

Then he heard his brother muttering something
about a quadrille and a galop; after which he began
to make some 'strange motions with his hands.

Cousin Hans received the impression that he was
trying to snap his fingers; and presently Ola said,
slowly, and clearly, in his monotonous and unsympathetic speaking voice: "Hope's clad in April
green— trommelommelom, trommelommelom:" you
see, poor fellow, he could not sing.

AT THE FAIR.

AT THE FAIR.

It was by the merest chance that Monsieur and Madame Tousseau came to Saint-Germain-en-Laye in the early days of September.

Four weeks ago they had been married in Lyons, which was their home ; but where they had passed these four weeks they really could not have told you. The time had gone hop-skip-and-jump ; a couple of days had entirely slipped out of their reckoning, and, on the other hand, they remembered a little summer-house at Fontainebleau, where they had rested one evening, as clearly as if they had passed half their lives there.

Paris was, strictly speaking, the goal of their wedding-journey, and there they established themselves in a comfortable little *hôtel garni*. But the city was sultry and they could not rest ; so they rambled about among the small towns in the neighborhood, and found themselves, one Sunday at noon, in Saint-Germain.

" Monsieur and Madame have doubtless come to take part in the fête?" said the plump little landlady of the Hôtel Henri Quatre, as she ushered her guests up the steps.

The fête? They knew of no fête in the world except their own wedded happiness; but they did not say so to the landlady.

They soon learned that they had been lucky enough to drop into the very midst of the great and celebrated fair which is held every year, on the first Sunday of September, in the Forest of Saint-Germain.

The young couple were highly delighted with their good hap. It seemed as though Fortune followed at their heels, or rather ran ahead of them, to arrange surprises. After a delicious tête-à-tête dinner behind one of the clipped yew trees in the quaint garden, they took a carriage and drove off to the forest.

In the hotel garden, beside the little fountain in the middle of the lawn, sat a ragged condor which the landlord had bought to amuse his guests. It was attached to its perch by a good strong rope. But when the sun shone upon it with real warmth, it fell a-thinking of the snow-peaks of Peru, of mighty wing-strokes over the deep valleys — and then it forgot the rope.

Two vigorous strokes with its pinions would bring the rope up taut, and it would fall back upon the sward. There it would lie by the hour, then shake itself and clamber up to its little perch again.

When it turned its head to watch the happy pair,

Madame Tousseau burst into a fit of laughter at its melancholy mien.

The afternoon sun glimmered through the dense foliage of the interminable straight-ruled avenue that skirts the terrace. The young wife's veil fluttered aloft as they sped through the air, and wound itself right round Monsieur's head. It took a long time to put it in order again, and Madame's hat had to be adjusted ever so often. Then came the re-lighting of Monsieur's cigar, and that, too, was quite a business; for Madame's fan would always give a suspicious little flirt every time the match was lighted; then a penalty had to be paid, and that, again, took time.

The aristocratic English family which was passing the summer at Saint Germain was disturbed in its regulation walk by the passing of the gay little equipage. They raised their correct gray or blue eyes; there was neither contempt nor annoyance in their look—only the faintest shade of surprise. But the condor followed the carriage with its eyes, until it became a mere black speck at the vanishing-point of the straight-ruled interminable avenue.

"La joyeuse fête des Loges" is a genuine fair, with gingerbread cakes, sword-swallowers, and waffles piping hot. As the evening falls, colored lamps and Chinese lanterns are lighted around the venerable oak which stands in the middle of the fair-ground, and boys climb about among its topmost branches with maroons and Bengal lights.

Gentlemen of an inventive turn of mind go about
with lanterns on their hats, on their sticks, and
wherever they can possibly hang ; and the most
inventive of all strolls around with his sweetheart
under a great umbrella, with a lantern dangling
from each rib.

On the outskirts, bonfires are lighted ; fowls are
roasted on spits, while potatoes are cut into slices
and fried in dripping. Each aroma seems to have
its amateurs, for there are always people crowding
round ; but the majority stroll up and down the
long street of booths.

Monsieur and Madame Tousseau had plunged
into all the fun of the fair. They had gambled in
the most lucrative lottery in Europe, presided over
by a man who excelled in dubious witticisms. They
had seen the fattest goose in the world, and the
celebrated flea, "Bismarch," who could drive six
horses. Furthermore, they had purchased gingerbread, shot at a target for clay pipes and soft-boiled
eggs, and finally had danced a waltz in the spacious
dancing-tent.

They had never had such fun in their lives.
There were no great people there—at any rate, none
greater than themselves. As they did not know a
soul, they smiled to every one, and when they met
the same person twice they laughed and nodded to
him.

They were charmed with everything. They stood
outside the great circus and ballet marquees and

laughed at the shouting buffoons. Scraggy mountebanks performed on trumpets, and young girls with
well-floured shoulders smiled alluringly from the
platforms.

Monsieur Tousseau's purse was never at rest;
but they did not grow impatient of the perpetual
claims upon it. On the contrary, they only laughed
at the gigantic efforts these people would make to
earn—perhaps half a franc, or a few centimes.

Suddenly they encountered a face they knew.
It was a young American whom they had met at
the hotel in Paris.

"Well, Monsieur Whitmore!" cried Madame Tousseau, gayly, "here at last you've found a place where
you can't possibly help enjoying yourself."

"For my part," answered the American, slowly,
"I find no enjoyment in seeing the people who
haven't money making fools of themselves to please
the people who have."

"Oh, you're incorrigible!" laughed the young
wife. "But I must compliment you on the excellent French you are speaking to-day."

After exchanging a few more words, they lost
each other in the crowd; Mr. Whitmore was going
back to Paris immediately.

Madame Tousseau's compliment was quite sincere. As a rule the grave American talked deplor-
able French, but the answer he had made to Madame was almost correct. It seemed as though it
had been well thought out in advance —as though

a whole series of impressions had condensed themselves into these words. Perhaps that was why
his answer sank so deep into the minds of Monsieur and Madame Tousseau.

Neither of them thought it a particularly brilliant
remark ; on the contrary, they agreed that it must
be miserable to take so gloomy a view of things.
But, nevertheless, his words left something rankling.
They could not laugh so lightly as before, Madame
felt tired, and they began to think of getting home-
wards.

Just as they turned to go down the long street
of booths in order to find their carriage, they met
a noisy crew coming upward.

"Let us take the other way," said Monsieur.

They passed between two booths, and emerged
at the back of one of the rows. They stumbled
over the tree-roots before their eyes got used to
the uncertain light which fell in patches between
the tents. A dog, which lay gnawing at something
or other, rose with a snarl, and dragged its prey
further into the darkness, among the trees.

On this side the booths were made up of old
sails and all sorts of strange draperies. Here and
there light shone through the openings, and at
one place Madame distinguished a face she knew.

It was the man who had sold her that incomparable gingerbread—Monsieur had half of it still
in his pocket.

But it was curious to see the gingerbread-man

from this side. Here was something quite different from the smiling obsequiousness which had said so many pretty things to her pretty face, and had been so unwearied in belauding the gingerbread —which really was excellent.

Now he sat crouched together, eating some indescribable mess out of a checked pocket-handkerchief—eagerly, greedily, without looking up.

Farther down they heard a muffled conversation. Madame was bent upon peeping in ; Monsieur objected, but he had to give in.

An old mountebank sat counting a handful of coppers, grumbling and growling the while. A young girl stood before him, shivering and pleading for pardon ; she was wrapped in a long water-proof.

The man swore, and stamped on the ground. Then she threw off the water-proof and stood half naked in a sort of ballet costume. Without saying a word, and without smoothing her hair or preening her finery, she mounted the little steps that led to the stage.

At that moment she turned and looked at her father. Her face had already put on the ballet-simper, but it now gave place to a quite different expression. The mouth remained fixed, but the eyes tried, for a second, to send him a beseeching smile. The mountebank shrugged his shoulders, and held out his hand with the coppers ; the girl turned, ducked under the curtain, and was received with shouts and applause.

Beside the great oak-tree the lottery man was holding forth as fluently as ever. His witticisms, as the darkness thickened, grew less and less dubious. There was a different ring, too, in the laughter of the crowd; the men were noisier, the mountebanks leaner, the women more brazen, the music falser—so it seemed, at least, to Madame and Monsieur.

As they passed the dancing-tent the racket of a quadrille reached their ears. "Great heavens!—was it really there that we danced?" said Madame, and nestled closer to her husband.

They made their way through the rout as quickly as they could; they would soon reach their carriage, it was just beyond the circus-marquee. It would be nice to rest and escape from all this hubbub.

The platform in front of the circus-marquee was now vacant. Inside, in the dim and stifling rotunda, the performance was in full swing.

Only the old woman who sold the tickets sat asleep at her desk. And a little way off, in the light of her lamp, stood a tiny boy.

He was dressed in tights, green on one side, red on the other; on his head he had a fool's cap with horns.

Close up to the platform stood a woman wrapped in a black shawl. She seemed to be talking to the boy.

He advanced his red leg and his green leg by

turns, and drew them back again. At last he took three steps forward on his meagre shanks and held out his hand to the woman.

She took what he had in it, and disappeared into the darkness.

He stood motionless for a moment, then he muttered some words and burst into tears.

Presently he stopped, and said: "Maman m'a pris mon sou!"—and fell to weeping again.

He dried his eyes and left off for a time, but as often as he repeated to himself his sad little history —how his mother had taken his sou from him—he was seized with another and a bitterer fit of weeping.

He stooped and buried his face in the curtain. The stiff, wrinkly oil-painting must be hard and cold to cry into. The little body shrank together; he drew his green leg close up under him, and stood like a stork upon the red one.

No one on the other side of the curtain must hear that he was crying. Therefore he did not sob like a child, but fought as a man fights against a broken heart.

When the attack was over, he blew his nose with his fingers, and wiped them on his tights. With the dirty curtain he had dabbled the tears all over his face until it was streaked with black; and in this guise, and dry-eyed, he gazed for a moment over the fair.

Then: "Maman m'a pris mon sou"—and he set off again.

The backsweep of the wave leaves the beach dry
for an instant while the next wave is gathering.
Thus sorrow swept in heavy surges over the little
childish heart.

His dress was so ludicrous, his body so meagre,
his weeping was so wofully bitter, and his suffering so great and man-like —

—But at home at the hotel—the Pavillon Henri
Quatre, where the Queens of France condescended
to be brought to bed—there the condor sat and
slept upon its perch.

And it dreamed its dream—its only dream—its
dream about the snow-peaks of Peru and the mighty
wing - strokes over the deep valleys; and then it
forgot its rope.

It uplifted its ragged pinions vigorously, and
struck two sturdy strokes. Then the rope drew taut,
and it fell back where it was wont to fall — it
wrenched its claw, and the dream vanished.—

—Next morning the aristocratic English family
was much concerned, and the landlord himself felt
annoyed, for the condor lay dead upon the grass.

TWO FRIENDS.

TWO FRIENDS.

No one could understand where he got his money from. But the person who marvelled most at the dashing and luxurious life led by Alphonse was his quondam friend and partner.

After they dissolved partnership, most of the custom and the best connection passed by degrees into Charles's hands. This was not because he in any way sought to run counter to his former partner; on the contrary, it arose simply from the fact that Charles was the more capable man of the two. And as Alphonse had now to work on his own account, it was soon clear to any one who observed him closely, that in spite of his promptitude, his amiability and his prepossessing appearance, he was not fitted to be at the head of an independent business.

And there was one person who *did* observe him closely. Charles followed him step by step with his sharp eyes; every blunder, every extravagance, every loss—he knew all to a nicety, and he wondered that Alphonse could keep going so long.

—They had as good as grown up together. Their mothers were cousins; the families had lived near each other in the same street; and in a city like Paris proximity is as important as relationship in promoting close intercourse. Moreover, the boys went to the same school.

Thenceforth, as they grew up to manhood, they were inseparable. Mutual adaptation overcame the great differences which originally marked their characters, until at last their idiosyncrasies fitted into each other like the artfully-carved pieces of wood which compose the picture-puzzles of our childhood.

The relation between them was really a beautiful one, such as does not often arise between two young men; for they did not understand friendship as binding the one to bear everything at the hands of the other, but seemed rather to vie with each other in mutual considerateness.

If, however, Alphonse in his relation to Charles showed any high degree of considerateness, he himself was ignorant of it; and if any one had told him of it he would doubtless have laughed loudly at such a mistaken compliment.

For as life on the whole appeared to him very simple and straightforward, the idea that his friendship should in any way fetter him was the last thing that could enter his head. That Charles was his best friend seemed to him as entirely natural as that he himself danced best, rode best, was the best shot, and that the whole world was ordered entirely to his mind.

Alphonse was in the highest degree a spoilt child of fortune ; he acquired everything without effort ; existence fitted him like an elegant dress, and he wore it with such unconstrained amiability that people forgot to envy him.

And then he was so handsome. He was tall and slim, with brown hair and big open eyes ; his complexion was clear and smooth, and his teeth shone when he laughed. He was quite conscious of his beauty, but, as everybody had petted him from his earliest days, his vanity was of a cheerful, good-natured sort, which, after all, was not so offensive. He was exceedingly fond of his friend. He amused himself and sometimes others by teasing him and making fun of him ; but he knew Charles's face so thoroughly that he saw at once when the jest was going too far. Then he would resume his natural, kindly tone, until he made the serious and somewhat melancholy Charles laugh till he was ill.

From his boyhood Charles had admired Alphonse beyond measure. He himself was small and insignificant, quiet and shy. His friend's brilliant qualities cast a lustre over him as well, and gave a certain impetus to his life.

His mother often said : "This friendship between the boys is a real blessing for my poor Charles, for without it he would certainly have been a melancholy creature."

When Alphonse was on all occasions preferred to him, Charles rejoiced; he was proud of his friend. He wrote his exercises, prompted him at examination, pleaded his cause with the masters, and fought for him with the boys.

At the commercial academy it was the same story. Charles worked for Alphonse, and Alphonse rewarded him with his inexhaustible amiability and unfailing good-humor.

When subsequently, as quite young men, they were placed in the same banker's office, it happened one day that the principal said to Charles: "From the first of May I will raise your salary."

"I thank you," answered Charles, "both on my own and on my friend's behalf."

"Monsieur Alphonse's salary remains unaltered," replied the chief, and went on writing.

Charles never forgot that morning. It was the first time he had been preferred or distinguished before his friend. And it was his commercial capacity, the quality which, as a young man of business, he valued most, that had procured him this preference; and it was the head of the firm, the great financier, who had himself accorded him such recognition.

The experience was so strange to him that it seemed like an injustice to his friend. He told Alphonse nothing of the occurrence; on the contrary, he proposed that they should apply for two vacant places in the Crédit Lyonnais.

Alphonse was quite willing, for he loved change, and the splendid new banking establishment on the Boulevard seemed to him far more attractive than the dark offices in the Rue Bergère. So they removed to the Crédit Lyonnais on the first of May. But as they were in the chief's office taking their leave, the old banker said to Charles, when Alphonse had gone out (Alphonse always took precedence of Charles), "Sentiment won't do for a business man."

From that day forward a change went on in Charles. He not only worked as industriously and conscientiously as before, but developed such energy and such an amazing faculty for labor as soon attracted to him the attention of his superiors. That he was far ahead of his friend in business capacity was soon manifest; but every time he received a new mark of recognition he had a struggle with himself. For a long time, every advancement brought with it a certain qualm of conscience; and yet he worked on with restless ardor.

One day Alphonse said, in his light, frank way: "You are really a smart fellow, Charlie! You're getting ahead of everybody, young and old—not to mention me. I'm quite proud of you!"

Charles felt ashamed. He had been thinking that Alphonse must feel wounded at being left on one side, and now he learned that his friend not only did not grudge him his advancement, but was even proud of him. By degrees his conscience was lulled to rest, and his solid worth was more and more appreciated—

But if he was in reality the more capable, how came it that he was so entirely ignored in society, while Alphonse remained everybody's darling? The very promotions and marks of appreciation which he had won for himself by hard work, were accorded him in a dry, business manner; while every one, from the directors to the messengers, had a friendly word or a merry greeting for Alphonse.

In the different offices and departments of the bank they intrigued to obtain possession of Monsieur Alphonse; for a breath of life and freshness followed ever in the wake of his handsome person and joyous nature. Charles, on the other hand, had often remarked that his colleagues regarded him as a dry person, who thought only of business and of himself.

The truth was that he had a heart of rare sensitiveness, with no faculty for giving it expression.

Charles was one of those small, black Frenchmen whose beard begins right under the eyes; his complexion was yellowish and his hair stiff and splintery. His eyes did not dilate when he was pleased and animated, but they flashed around and glittered. When he laughed the corners of his mouth turned upward, and many a time, when his heart was full of joy and good-will, he had seen people draw back, half-frightened by his forbidding exterior. Alphonse

alone knew him so well that he never seemed to
see his ugliness; every one else misunderstood him.
He became suspicious, and retired more and more
within himself.

In an insensible crescendo the thought grew in
him: Why should he never attain anything of that
which he most longed for—intimate and cordial intercourse and friendliness which should answer to
the warmth pent up within him? Why should every
one smile to Alphonse with out-stretched hands,
while he must content himself with stiff bows and
cold glances!

Alphonse knew nothing of all this. He was joyous and healthy, charmed with life and content with
his daily work. He had been placed in the easiest
and most interesting branch of the business, and,
with his quick brain and his knack of making himself agreeable, he filled his place satisfactorily.

His social circle was very large—every one set
store by his acquaintance, and he was at least as
popular among women as among men.

For a time Charles accompanied Alphonse into
society, until he was seized by a misgiving that he
was invited for his friend's sake alone, when he at
once drew back.

When Charles proposed that they should set up
in business together, Alphonse had answered: "It
is too good of you to choose me. You could easily
find a much better partner."

Charles had imagined that their altered relations

and closer association in work would draw Alphonse out of the circles which Charles could not now endure, and unite them more closely. For he had conceived a vague dread of losing his friend.

He did not himself know, nor would it have been easy to decide, whether he was jealous of all the people who flocked around Alphonse and drew him to them, or whether he envied his friend's popularity.

—They began their business prudently and energetically, and got on well.

It was generally held that each formed an admirable complement to the other. Charles represented the solid, confidence-inspiring element, while the handsome and elegant Alphonse imparted to the firm a certain lustre which was far from being without value.

Every one who came into the counting-house at once remarked his handsome figure, and thus it seemed quite natural that all should address themselves to him.

Charles meanwhile bent over his work and let Alphonse be spokesman. When Alphonse asked him about anything, he answered shortly and quietly without looking up.

Thus most people thought that Charles was a confidential clerk, while Alphonse was the real head of the house.

As Frenchmen, they thought little about marrying, but as young Parisians they led a life into which erotics entered largely.

Alphonse was never really in his element except when in female society. Then all his exhilarating amiability came into play, and when he leaned back at supper and held out his shallow champagne-glass to be refilled, he was as beautiful as a happy god.

He had a neck of the kind which women long to caress, and his soft, half-curling hair looked as if it were negligently arranged, or carefully disarranged, by a woman's coquettish hand.

Indeed, many slim white fingers had passed through those locks; for Alphonse had not only the gift of being loved by women, but also the yet rarer gift of being forgiven by them.

When the friends were together at gay supper-parties, Alphonse paid no particular heed to Charles. He kept no account of his own love-affairs, far less of those of his friend. So it might easily happen that a beauty on whom Charles had cast a longing eye fell into the hands of Alphonse.

Charles was used to seeing his friend preferred in life; but there are certain things to which men can scarcely accustom themselves. He seldom went with Alphonse to his suppers, and it was always long before the wine and the general exhilaration could bring him into a convivial humor.

But then, when the champagne and the bright eyes had gone to his head, he would often be the wildest of all; he would sing loudly with his harsh voice, laugh and gesticulate so that his stiff

black hair fell over his forehead; and then the
merry ladies shrank from him, and called him the
"chimney-sweep."

—As the sentry paces up and down in the be-
leaguered fortress, he sometimes hears a strange
sound in the silent night, as if something were
rustling under his feet. It is the enemy, who has
undermined the outworks, and to-night or to-morrow night there will be a hollow explosion, and
armed men will storm in through the breach.

If Charles had kept close watch over himself he
would have heard strange thoughts rustling within him. But he would not hear—he had only a
dim foreboding that some time there must come an
explosion.

—And one day it came.

It was already after business hours; the clerks
had all left the outer office, and only the principals
remained behind.

Charles was busily writing a letter which he
wished to finish before he left.

Alphonse had drawn on both his gloves and buttoned them. Then he had brushed his hat until it
shone, and now he was walking up and down and
peeping into Charles's letter every time he passed
the desk.

They used to spend an hour every day before
dinner in a café on the great Boulevard, and
Alphonse was getting impatient for his newspa-
pers.

"Will you never have finished that letter?" he said, rather irritably.

Charles was silent a second or two, then he sprang up so that his chair fell over: "Perhaps Alphonse imagined that he could do it better? Did he not know which of them was really the man of business?" And now the words streamed out with that incredible rapidity of which the French language is capable when it is used in fiery passion.

But it was a turbid stream, carrying with it many ugly expressions, upbraidings and recriminations; and through the whole there sounded something like a suppressed sob.

As he strode up and down the room, with clenched hands and dishevelled hair, Charles looked like a little wiry-haired terrier barking at an elegant Italian greyhound. At last he seized his hat and rushed out.

Alphonse had stood looking at him with great wondering eyes. When he was gone, and there was once more silence in the room, it seemed as though the air was still quivering with the hot words. Alphonse recalled them one by one, as he stood motionless beside the desk.

"Did he not know which was the abler of the two?" Yes, assuredly! he had never denied that Charles was by far his superior.

"He must not think that he would succeed in winning everything to himself with his smooth face." Alphonse was not conscious of ever having deprived his friend of anything.

" I don't care for your *cocottes*," Charles had said.

Could he really have been interested in the little Spanish dancer? If Alphonse had only had the faintest suspicion of such a thing he would never have looked at her. But that was nothing to get so wild about; there were plenty of women in Paris.

And at last: "As sure as to morrow comes, I will dissolve partnership!"

Alphonse did not understand it at all. He left the counting-house and walked moodily through the streets until he met an acquaintance. That put other thoughts into his head; but all day he had a feeling as if something gloomy and uncomfortable lay in wait, ready to seize him so soon as he was alone.

When he reached home, late at night, he found a letter from Charles. He opened it hastily; but it contained, instead of the apology he had expected, only a coldly-worded request to M. Alphonse to attend at the counting-house early the next morning " in order that the contemplated dissolution of partnership might be effected as quickly as possible."

Now, for the first time, did Alphonse begin to understand that the scene in the counting-house had been more than a passing outburst of passion; but this only made the affair more inexplicable.

And the longer he thought it over, the more

clearly did he feel that Charles had been unjust to
him. He had never been angry with his friend,
nor was he precisely angry even now. But as he
repeated to himself all the insults Charles had
heaped upon him, his good-natured heart hardened ;
and the next morning he took his place in silence,
after a cold " Good-morning."

Although he arrived a whole hour earlier than
usual, he could see that Charles had been working
long and industriously. There they sat, each on
his side of the desk ; they spoke only the most indispensable words ; now and then a paper passed
from hand to hand, but they never looked each
other in the face.

In this way they both worked—each more busily
than the other—until twelve o'clock, their usual
luncheon-time.

This hour of *déjeûner* was the favorite time of
both. Their custom was to have it served in their
office, and when the old house-keeper announced
that lunch was ready, they would both rise at once,
even if they were in the midst of a sentence or of
an account.

They used to eat standing by the fireplace or
walking up and down in the warm, comfortable
office. Alphonse had always some piquant stories
to tell, and Charles laughed at them. These were
his pleasantest hours.

But that day, when Madame said her friendly
"*Messieurs, on a servi,*" they both remained sitting.

She opened her eyes wide, and repeated the words as she went out, but neither moved.

At last Alphonse felt hungry, went to the table, poured out a glass of wine and began to eat his cutlet. But as he stood there eating, with his glass in his hand, and looked round the dear old office where they had spent so many pleasant hours, and then thought that they were to lose all this and imbitter their lives for a whim, a sudden burst of passion, the whole situation appeared to him so preposterous that he almost burst out laughing.

"Look here, Charles," he said, in the half-earnest, half-joking tone which always used to make Charles laugh, "it will really be too absurd to advertise: 'According to an amicable agreement, from such and such a date the firm of——' "

"I have been thinking," interrupted Charles, quietly, "that we will put: 'According to *mutual* agreement.' "

Alphonse laughed no more; he put down his glass, and the cutlet tasted bitter in his mouth.

He understood that friendship was dead between them, why or wherefore he could not tell; but he thought that Charles was hard and unjust to him. He was now stiffer and colder than the other.

They worked together until the business of dissolution was finished; then they parted.

A considerable time passed, and the two quondam friends worked each in his own quarter in the great Paris. They met at the Bourse, but never did business with each other. Charles never worked against Alphonse; he did not wish to ruin him; he wished Alphonse to ruin himself.

And Alphonse seemed likely enough to meet his friend's wishes in this respect. It is true that now and then he did a good stroke of business, but the steady industry he had learned from Charles he soon forgot. He began to neglect his office, and lost many good connections.

He had always had a taste for dainty and luxurious living, but his association with the frugal Charles had hitherto held his extravagances in check. Now, on the contrary, his life became more and more dissipated. He made fresh acquaintances on every hand, and was more than ever the brilliant and popular Monsieur Alphonse; but Charles kept an eye on his growing debts.

He had Alphonse watched as closely as possible, and, as their business was of the same kind, could form a pretty good estimate of the other's earnings. His expenses were even easier to ascertain, and he soon assured himself of the fact that Alphonse was beginning to run into debt in several quarters.

He cultivated some acquaintances about whom he otherwise cared nothing, merely because through them he got an insight into Alphonse's expensive mode of life and rash prodigality. He sought the same cafés and restaurants as Alphonse, but at

7

different times; he even had his clothes made by the same tailor, because the talkative little man entertained him with complaints that Monsieur Alphonse never paid his bills.

Charles often thought how easy it would be to buy up a part of Alphonse's liabilities and let them fall into the hands of a grasping usurer. But it would be a great injustice to suppose that Charles for a moment contemplated doing such a thing himself. It was only an idea he was fond of dwelling upon; he was, as it were, in love with Alphonse's debts.

But things went slowly, and Charles became pale and sallow while he watched and waited.

He was longing for the time when the people who had always looked down upon him should have their eyes opened, and see how little the brilliant and idolized Alphonse was really fit for. He wanted to see him humbled, abandoned by his friends, lonely and poor; and then—!

Beyond that he really did not like to speculate; for at this point feelings stirred within him which he would not acknowledge.

He *would* hate his former friend; he *would* have revenge for all the coldness and neglect which had been his own lot in life; and every time the least thought in defence of Alphonse arose in his mind he pushed it aside, and said, like the old banker: "Sentiment won't do for a business man."

One day he went to his tailor's; he bought

more clothes in these days than he absolutely needed.

The nimble little man at once ran to meet him with a roll of cloth : " See, here is the very stuff for you. Monsieur Alphonse has had a whole suit made of it, and Monsieur Alphonse is a gentleman who knows how to dress."

" I did not think that Monsieur Alphonse was one of your favorite customers," said Charles, rather taken by surprise.

" Oh, *mon Dieu!*" exclaimed the little tailor, " you mean because I have once or twice mentioned that Monsieur Alphonse owed me a few thousand francs. It was very stupid of me to speak so. Monsieur Alphonse has not only paid me the trifle he was owing, but I know that he has also satisfied a number of other creditors. I have done *ce cher beau monsieur* great injustice, and I beg you never to give him a hint of my stupidity."

Charles was no longer listening to the chatter of the garrulous tailor. He soon left the shop, and went up the street quite absorbed in the one thought that Alphonse had paid.

He thought how foolish it really was of him to wait and wait for the other's ruin. How easily might not the adroit and lucky Alphonse come across many a brilliant business opening, and make plenty of money without a word of it reaching Charles's ears. Perhaps, after all, he was getting on well. Perhaps it would end in people saying:

" See, at last Monsieur Alphonse shows what he is
fit for, now that he is quit of his dull and crabbed
partner !"

Charles went slowly up the street with his head
bent. Many people jostled him, but he heeded not.
His life seemed to him so meaningless, as if he had
lost all that he had ever possessed—or had he himself cast it from him? Just then some one ran
against him with more than usual violence. He
looked up. It was an acquaintance from the time
when he and Alphonse had been in the Crédit Lyonnais.

" Ah, good-day, Monsieur Charles !" cried he,
" It is long since we met. Odd, too, that I should
meet you to-day. I was just thinking of you this
morning."

" Why, may I ask ?" said Charles, half-absently.

" Well, you see, only to-day I saw up at the bank
a paper—a bill for thirty or forty thousand francs—
bearing both your name and that of Monsieur Alphonse. It astonished me, for I thought that you
two—hm !—had done with each other."

" No, we have not quite done with each other
yet," said Charles, slowly.

He struggled with all his might to keep his face
calm, and asked in as natural a tone as he could
command : " When does the bill fall due ? I don't
quite recollect."

" To-morrow or the day after, I think," answered
the other, who was a hard-worked business man,

and was already in a hurry to be off. "It was accepted by Monsieur Alphonse."

"I know that," said Charles; "but could you not manage to let *me* redeem the bill to-morrow? It is a courtesy—a favor I am anxious to do."

"With pleasure. Tell your messenger to ask for me personally at the bank to-morrow afternoon. I will arrange it; nothing easier. Excuse me; I'm in a hurry. Good-bye!" and with that he ran on—

—Next day Charles sat in his counting-house waiting for the messenger who had gone up to the bank to redeem Alphonse's bill.

At last a clerk entered, laid a folded blue paper by his principal's side, and went out again.

Not until the door was closed did Charles seize the draft, look swiftly round the room, and open it. He stared for a second or two at his name, then lay back in his chair and drew a deep breath. It was as he had expected—the signature was a forgery.

He bent over it again. For long he sat, gazing at his own name, and observing how badly it was counterfeited.

While his sharp eye followed every line in the letters of his name, he scarcely thought. His mind was so disturbed, and his feelings so strangely conflicting, that it was some time before he became conscious how much they betrayed—these bungling strokes on the blue paper.

He felt a strange lump in his throat, his nose be-

gan to tickle a little, and, before he was aware of it,
a big tear fell on the paper.

He looked hastily around, took out his pocket-
handkerchief, and carefully wiped the wet place on
the bill. He thought again of the old banker in
the Rue Bergère.

What did it matter to him that Alphonse's weak
character had at last led him to crime, and what
had he lost? Nothing, for did he not hate his
former friend? No one could say it was his fault
that Alphonse was ruined—he had shared with him
honestly, and never harmed him.

Then his thoughts turned to Alphonse. He knew
him well enough to be sure that when the refined,
delicate Alphonse had sunk so low, he must have
come to a jutting headland in life, and be prepared
to leap out of it rather than let disgrace reach him.

At this thought Charles sprang up. That must
not be. Alphonse should not have time to send a
bullet through his head and hide his shame in the
mixture of compassion and mysterious horror which
follows the suicide. Thus Charles would lose his
revenge, and it would be all to no purpose that he
had gone and nursed his hatred until he himself
had become evil through it. Since he had forever
lost his friend, he would at least expose his enemy,
so that all should see what a miserable, despicable
being was this charming Alphonse.

He looked at his watch; it was half-past four.
Charles knew the café in which he would find Al-

phonse at this hour; he pocketed the bill and buttoned his coat.

But on the way he would call at a police-station,
and hand over the bill to a detective, who at a sign
from Charles should suddenly advance into the
middle of the café where Alphonse was always sur-
rounded by his friends and admirers, and say loudly and distinctly so that all should hear it:

"Monsieur Alphonse, you are charged with forgery."

It was raining in Paris. The day had been fog-
gy, raw, and cold; and well on in the afternoon it
had begun to rain. It was not a downpour—the
water did not fall from the clouds in regular
drops—but the clouds themselves had, as it were,
laid themselves down in the streets of Paris and
there slowly condensed into water.

No matter how people might seek to shelter
themselves, they got wet on all sides. The moist-
ure slid down the back of your neck, laid itself like
a wet towel about your knees, penetrated into your
boots and far up your trousers.

A few sanguine ladies were standing in the *portes
cochères*, with their skirts tucked up, expecting it to
clear; others waited by the hour in the omnibus
stations. But most of the stronger sex hurried
along under their umbrellas: only a few had been
sensible enough to give up the battle, and had
turned up their collars, stuck their umbrellas

under their arms, and their hands in their pockets.

Although it was early in the autumn it was already dusk at five o'clock. A few gas-jets lighted in the narrowest streets, and in a shop here and there, strove to shine out in the thick wet air.

People swarmed as usual in the streets, jostled one another off the pavement, and ruined one another's umbrellas. All the cabs were taken up; they splashed along and bespattered the foot-passengers to the best of their ability, while the asphalte glistened in the dim light with a dense coating of mud.

The cafés were crowded to excess: regular customers went round and scolded, and the waiters ran against each other in their hurry. Ever and anon, amid the confusion, could be heard the sharp little ting of the bell on the buffet; it was *la dame du comptoir* summoning a waiter, while her calm eyes kept a watch upon the whole café.

A lady sat at the buffet of a large restaurant on the Boulevard Sebastopol. She was widely known for her cleverness and her amiable manners.

She had glossy black hair, which, in spite of the fashion, she wore parted in the middle of her forehead in natural curls. Her eyes were almost black and her mouth full, with a little shadow of a mustache.

Her figure was still very pretty, although, if the truth were known, she had probably passed her thirtieth year; and she had a soft little hand, with

which she wrote elegant figures in her cash-book,
and now and then a little note. Madame Virginie
could converse with the young dandies who were
always hanging about the buffet, and parry their
witticisms, while she kept account with the waiters
and had her eye upon every corner of the great
room.

She was really pretty only from five till seven in
the afternoon — that being the time at which Alphonse invariably visited the café. Then her eyes
never left him; she got a fresher color, her mouth
was always trembling into a smile, and her movements became somewhat nervous. That was the
only time of the day when she was ever known to
give a random answer or to make a mistake in
the accounts; and the waiters tittered and nudged
each other.

For it was generally thought that she had formerly had relations with Alphonse, and some would
even have it that she was still his mistress.

She herself best knew how matters stood; but it
was impossible to be angry with Monsieur Alphonse.
She was well aware that he cared no more for her
than for twenty others; that she had lost him—nay,
that he had never really been hers. And yet her
eyes besought a friendly look, and when he left the
café without sending her a confidential greeting, it
seemed as though she suddenly faded, and the waiters said to each other: "Look at Madame; she is
gray to-night"—

—Over at the windows it was still light enough
to read the papers; a couple of young men were
amusing themselves with watching the crowds which
streamed past.   Seen through the great plate-glass
windows, the busy forms gliding past one another
in the dense, wet, rainy air looked like fish in an
aquarium.   Farther back in the café, and over the
bililard-tables, the gas was lighted.   Alphonse was
playing with a couple of friends.

He had been to the buffet and greeted Madame
Virginie, and she, who had long noticed how Alphonse was growing paler day by day, had—half
in jest, half in anxiety—reproached him with his
thoughtless life.

Alphonse answered with a poor joke and asked
for absinthe.

How she hated those light ladies of the ballet
and the opera who enticed Monsieur Alphonse to
revel night after night at the gaming-table, or at
interminable suppers!   How ill he had been looking these last few weeks!   He had grown quite
thin, and the great gentle eyes had acquired a pierc-
ing, restless look.   What would she not give to be
able to rescue him out of that life that was dragging
him down!   She glanced in the opposite mirror
and thought she had beauty enough left.

Now and then the door opened and a new guest
came in, stamped his feet and shut his wet umbrella.   All bowed to Madame Virginie, and almost
all said, "What horrible weather!"

When Charles entered he saluted shortly and took a seat in the corner beside the fireplace.

Alphonse's eyes had indeed become restless. He looked towards the door every time any one came in; and when Charles appeared, a spasm passed over his face and he missed his stroke.

"Monsieur Alphonse is not in the vein to-day," said an onlooker.

Soon after a strange gentleman came in. Charles looked up from his paper and nodded slightly; the stranger raised his eyebrows a little and looked at Alphonse.

He dropped his cue on the floor.

"Excuse me, gentlemen, I'm not in the mood for billiards to-day," said he, "permit me to leave off. Waiter, bring me a bottle of seltzer-water and a spoon—I must take my dose of Vichy salts."

"You should not take so much Vichy salts, Monsieur Alphonse, but rather keep to a sensible diet," said the doctor, who sat a little way off playing chess.

Alphonse laughed, and seated himself at the newspaper-table. He seized the *Journal Amusant*, and began to make merry remarks upon the illustrations. A little circle quickly gathered round him, and he was inexhaustible in racy stories and whimsicalities.

While he rattled on under cover of the others' laughter, he poured out a glass of seltzer-water and took from his pocket a little box on which was written, in large letters, "Vichy Salts."

He shook the powder out into the glass and stirred it round with a spoon. There was a little cigar-ash on the floor in front of his chair; he whipped it off with his pocket-handkerchief, and then stretched out his hand for the glass.

At that moment he felt a hand on his arm. Charles had risen and hurried across the room; he now bent down over Alphonse.

Alphonse turned his head towards him so that none but Charles could see his face. At first he let his eyes travel furtively over his old friend's figure; then he looked up, and, gazing straight at Charles, he said, half aloud, " Charlie!"

It was long since Charles had heard that old pet name. He gazed into the well-known face, and now for the first time saw how it had altered of late. It seemed to him as though he were reading a tragic story about himself.

They remained thus for a second or two, and there glided over Alphonse's features that expression of imploring helplessness which Charles knew so well from the old school-days, when Alphonse came bounding in at the last moment and wanted his composition written.

"Have you done with the *Journal Amusant?*" asked Charles, with a thick utterance.

"Yes; pray take it." answered Alphonse, hurriedly. He reached him the paper, and at the same time got hold of Charles's thumb. He pressed it and whispered, "Thanks," then—drained the glass.

Charles went over to the stranger who sat by the door : " Give me the bill."

" You don't need our assistance, then ?"

" No, thanks."

" So much the better," said the stranger, handing Charles a folded blue paper. Then he paid for his coffee and went.—

—Madame Virginie rose with a little shriek : " Alphonse ! Oh, my God ! Monsieur Alphonse is ill."

He slipped off his chair ; his shoulders went up and his head fell on one side. He remained sitting on the floor, with his back against the chair.

There was a movement among those nearest ; the doctor sprang over and knelt beside him. When he looked in Alphonse's face he started a little. He took his hand as if to feel his pulse, and at the same time bent down over the glass which stood on the edge of the table.

With a movement of the arm he gave it a slight push, so that it fell on the floor and was smashed. Then he laid down the dead man's hand and bound a handkerchief round his chin.

Not till then did the others understand what had happened. " Dead? Is he dead, doctor? Monsieur Alphonse dead ?"

" Heart disease," answered the doctor.

One came running with water, another with vinegar. Amid laughter and noise, the balls could be heard cannoning on the inner billiard-table.

"Hush!" some one whispered. "Hush!" was repeated ; and the silence spread in wider and wider circles round the corpse, until all was quite still.

"Come and lend a hand," said the doctor.

The dead man was lifted up ; they laid him on a sofa in a corner of the room, and the nearest gas-jets were put out.

Madame Virginie was still standing up ; her face was chalk-white, and she held her little soft hand pressed against her breast. They carried him right past the buffet. The doctor had seized him under the back, so that his waistcoat slipped up and a piece of his fine white shirt appeared.

She followed with her eyes the slender, supple limbs she knew so well, and continued to stare towards the dark corner.

Most of the guests went away in silence. A couple of young men entered noisily from the street ; a waiter ran towards them and said a few words. They glanced towards the corner, buttoned their coats, and plunged out again into the fog.

The half-darkened café was soon empty ; only some of Alphonse's nearest friends stood in a group and whispered. The doctor was talking with the proprietor, who had now appeared on the scene.

The waiters stole to and fro making great circuits to avoid the dark corner. One of them knelt and gathered up the fragments of the glass on a tray. He did his work as quietly as he could ; but for all that it made too much noise.

"Let that alone until by-and-by," said the host, softly.

—Leaning against the chimney-piece, Charles looked at the dead man. He slowly tore the folded paper to pieces, while he thought of his friend—

A GOOD CONSCIENCE.

A GOOD CONSCIENCE.

AN elegant little carriage, with two sleek and well-fed horses, drew up at Advocate Abel's garden gate.

Neither silver nor any other metal was visible in the harness; everything was a dull black, and all the buckles were leather-covered. In the lacquering of the carriage there was a trace of dark green; the cushions were of a subdued dust-color; and only on close inspection could you perceive that the coverings were of the richest silk. The coachman looked like an English clergyman, in his close-buttoned black coat, with a little stand-up collar and stiff white necktie.

Mrs. Warden, who sat alone in the carriage, bent forward and laid her hand upon the ivory door-handle; then she slowly alighted, drew her long train after her, and carefully closed the carriage door.

You might have wondered that the coachman did not dismount to help her; the fat horses certainly did not look as though they would play any tricks if he dropped the reins.

But when you looked at his immovable countenance and his correct iron-gray whiskers, you understood at once that this was a man who knew what
he was doing, and never neglected a detail of his
duty.

Mrs. Warden passed through the little garden in
front of the house, and entered the garden-room.
The door to the adjoining room stood half open,
and there she saw the lady of the house at a large
table covered with rolls of light stuff and scattered
numbers of the *Bazar*.

"Ah, you've come just at the right moment, my
dear Emily!" cried Mrs. Abel, "I'm quite in despair over my dress-maker—she can't think of anything new. And here I'm sitting, ransacking the
Bazar. Take off your shawl, dear, and come and
help me ; it's a walking-dress."

"I'm afraid I'm scarcely the person to help you
in a matter of dress," answered Mrs. Warden.

Good-natured Mrs. Abel stared at her; there
was something disquieting in her tone, and she had
a vast respect for her rich friend.

"You remember I told you the other day that
Warden had promised me—that's to say" Mrs.
Warden corrected herself—"he had asked me to
order a new silk dress—"

"From Madame Labiche—of course!"—interrupted Mrs. Abel. "And I suppose you're on your
way to her now? Oh, take me with you! It will
be such fun!"

"I am not going to Madame Labiche's," answered Mrs. Warden, almost solemnly.

"Good gracious, why not?" asked her friend, while her good-humored brown eyes grew spherical with astonishment.

"Well, you must know," answered Mrs. Warden, "it seems to me we can't with a good conscience pay so much money for unnecessary finery, when we know that on the outskirts of the town—and even at our very doors—there are hundreds of people living in destitution—literally in destitution."

"Yes, but," objected the advocate's wife, casting an uneasy glance over her table, "isn't that the way of the world? We know that inequality—"

"We ought to be careful not to increase the inequality, but rather to do what we can to smooth it away," Mrs. Warden interrupted. And it appeared to Mrs. Abel that her friend cast a glance of disapprobation over the table, the stuffs, and the *Bazars*.

"It's only alpaca," she interjected, timidly.

"Good heavens, Caroline!" cried Mrs. Warden, "pray don't think that I'm reproaching you. These things depend entirely upon one's individual point of view—every one must follow the dictates of his own conscience."

The conversation continued for some time, and Mrs. Warden related that it was her intention to drive out to the very lowest of the suburbs, in order to assure herself, with her own eyes, of the conditions of life among the poor.

On the previous day she had read the annual
report of a private charitable society of which her
husband was a member. She had purposely re-
frained from applying to the police or the poor-law
authorities for information. It was the very gist of
her design personally to seek out poverty, to make
herself familiar with it, and then to render assistance.

The ladies parted a little less effusively than
usual. They were both in a serious frame of mind.

Mrs. Abel remained in the garden-room ; she felt
no inclination to set to work again at the walking-
dress, although the stuff was really pretty. She
heard the muffled sound of the carriage-wheels as
they rolled off over the smooth roadway of the villa
quarter.

" What a good heart Emily has," she sighed.

Nothing could be more remote than envy from
the good-natured lady's character ; and yet — it was
with a feeling akin to envy that she now followed
the light carriage with her eyes. But whether it
was her friend's good heart or her elegant equipage that she envied her it was not easy to say.

She had given the coachman his orders, which he
had received without moving a muscle : and as re-
monstrance was impossible to him, he drove deeper
and deeper into the queerest streets in the poor
quarter, with a countenance as though he were
driving to a Court ball.

At last he received orders to stop, and indeed it

was high time. For the street grew narrower and narrower, and it seemed as though the fat horses and the elegant carriage must at the very next moment have stuck fast, like a cork in the neck of a bottle.

The immovable one showed no sign of anxiety, although the situation was in reality desperate. A humorist, who stuck his head out of a garret window, went so far as to advise him to slaughter his horses on the spot, as they could never get out again alive.

Mrs. Warden alighted, and turned into a still narrower street; she wanted to see poverty at its very worst.

In a door-way stood a half-grown girl. Mrs. Warden asked: "Do very poor people live in this house?"

The girl laughed and made some answer as she brushed close past her in the narrow door-way. Mrs. Warden did not understand what she said, but she had an impression that it was something ugly.

She entered the first room she came to.

It was not a new idea to Mrs. Warden that poor people never keep their rooms properly ventilated. Nevertheless, she was so overpowered by the atmosphere she found herself inhaling that she was glad to sink down on a bench beside the stove.

Mrs. Warden was struck by something in the gesture with which the woman of the house swept down upon the floor the clothes which were lying on the bench, and in the smile with which she invited the fine lady to be seated. She received the impression that the poor woman had seen better days, although her movements were bouncing rather than refined, and her smile was far from pleasant.

The long train of Mrs. Warden's pearl-gray visiting dress spread over the grimy floor, and as she stooped and drew it to her she could not help thinking of an expression of Heine's, " She looked like a bon-bon which has fallen in the mire."

The conversation began, and was carried on as such conversations usually are. If each had kept to her own language and her own line of thought, neither of these two women would have understood a word that the other said.

But as the poor always know the rich much better than the rich know the poor, the latter have at last acquired a peculiar dialect—a particular tone which experience has taught them to use when they are anxious to make themselves understood— that is to say, understood in such a way as to incline the wealthy to beneficence. Nearer to each other they can never come.

Of this dialect the poor woman was a perfect mistress, and Mrs. Warden had soon a general idea of her miserable case. She had two children a boy of four or five, who was lying on the floor, and a baby at the breast.

Mrs. Warden gazed at the pallid little creature, and could not believe that it was thirteen months old. At home in his cradle she herself had a little colossus of seven months, who was at least half as big again as this child.

"You must give the baby something strengthening," she said; and she had visions of phosphate food and orange jelly.

At the words "something strengthening," a shaggy head looked up from the bedstraw; it belonged to a pale, hollow-eyed man with a large woollen comforter wrapped round his jaws.

Mrs. Warden was frightened. "Your husband?" she asked.

The poor woman answered yes, it was her husband. He had not gone to work to-day because he had such bad toothache.

Mrs. Warden had had toothache herself, and knew how painful it is. She uttered some words of sincere sympathy.

The man muttered something, and lay back again; and at the same moment Mrs. Warden discovered an inmate of the room whom she had not hitherto observed.

It was a quite young girl, who was seated in the corner at the other side of the stove. She stared for a moment at the fine lady, but quickly drew back her head and bent forward, so that the visitor could see little but her back.

Mrs. Warden thought the girl had some sewing

in her lap which she wanted to hide ; perhaps it was some old garment she was mending.

"Why does the big boy lie upon the floor?" asked Mrs. Warden.

"He's lame," answered the mother. And now followed a detailed account of the poor boy's case, with many lamentations. He had been attacked with hip-disease after the scarlet-fever.

"You must buy him—" began Mrs. Warden, intending to say, "a wheel-chair." But it occurred to her that she had better buy it herself. It is not wise to let poor people get too much money into their hands. But she would give the woman something at once. Here was real need, a genuine case for help ; and she felt in her pocket for her purse.

It was not there. How annoying—she must have left it in the carriage.

Just as she was turning to the woman to express her regret, and promise to send some money presently, the door opened, and a well-dressed gentleman entered. His face was very full, and of a sort of dry, mealy pallor.

"Mrs. Warden, I presume?" said the stranger. "I saw your carriage out in the street, and I have brought you this—your purse, is it not?"

Mrs. Warden looked at it—yes, certainly, it was hers, with E. W. inlaid in black on the polished ivory.

"I happened to see it, as I turned the corner, in the hands of a girl—one of the most disreputable in the quarter," the stranger explained; adding, " I am the poor-law inspector of the district."

Mrs. Warden thanked him, although she did not at all like his appearance. But when she again looked round the room she was quite alarmed by the change which had taken place in its occupants.

The husband sat upright in the bed and glared at the fat gentleman, the wife's face wore an ugly smile, and even the poor wee cripple had scrambled towards the door, and resting on his lean arms, stared upward like a little animal.

And in all these eyes there was the same hate, the same aggressive defiance. Mrs. Warden felt as though she were now separated by an immense interval from the poor woman with whom she had just been talking so openly and confidentially.

" So that's the state you're in to-day, Martin," said the gentleman, in quite a different voice. " I thought you'd been in that affair last night. Never mind, they're coming for you this afternoon. It'll be a two months' business."

All of a sudden the torrent was let loose. The man and woman shouted each other down, the girl behind the stove came forward and joined in, the cripple shrieked and rolled about. It was impossible to distinguish the words; but what between voices, eyes, and hands, it seemed as though the stuffy little room must fly asunder with all the wild passion exploding in it.

Mrs. Warden turned pale and rose, the gentleman

opened the door, and both hastened out. As she passed down the passage she heard a horrible burst of feminine laughter behind her. It must be the woman—the same woman who had spoken so softly and despondently about the poor children.

She felt half angry with the man who had brought about this startling change, and as they now walked side by side up the street she listened to him with a cold and distant expression.

But gradually her bearing changed : there was really so much in what he said.

The poor-law inspector told her what a pleasure it was to him to find a lady like Mrs. Warden so compassionate towards the poor. Though it was much to be deplored that even the most well-meant help so often came into unfortunate hands, yet there was always something fine and ennobling in seeing a lady like Mrs. Warden—

"But," she interrupted, "aren't these people in the utmost need of help? I received the impression that the woman in particular had seen better days, and that a little timely aid might perhaps enable her to recover herself."

"I am sorry to have to tell you, madam," said the poor-law inspector, in a tone of mild regret, "that she was formerly a very notorious woman of the town."

Mrs. Warden shuddered.

She had spoken to such a woman, and spoken about children. She had even mentioned her own child, lying at home in its innocent cradle. She almost felt as though she must hasten home to make sure it was still as clean and wholesome as before.

"And the young girl?" she asked, timidly.

"No doubt you noticed her—her condition."

"No. You mean—"

The fat gentleman whispered some words.

Mrs. Warden started: "By the man!—the man of the house?"

"Yes, madam, I am sorry to have to tell you so; but you can understand that these people—" and he whispered again.

This was too much for Mrs. Warden. She turned almost dizzy, and accepted the gentleman's arm. They now walked rapidly towards the carriage, which was standing a little farther off than the spot at which she had left it.

For the immovable one had achieved a feat which even the humorist had acknowledged with an elaborate oath.

After sitting for some time, stiff as a poker, he had backed his sleek horses, step by step, until they reached a spot where the street widened a little, though the difference was imperceptible to any other eyes than those of an accomplished coachman.

A whole pack of ragged children swarmed about the carriage, and did all they could to upset the composure of the sleek steeds. But the spirit of the immovable one was in them.

After having measured with a glance of perfect composure the distance between two flights of steps, one on each side of the street, he made the sleek pair turn, slowly and step by step, so short and sharp that it seemed as though the elegant carriage must be crushed to fragments, but so accurately that there was not an inch too much or too little on either side.

Now he once more sat stiff as a poker, still measuring with his eyes the distance between the steps. He even made a mental note of the number of a constable who had watched the feat, in order to have a witness to appeal to if his account of it should be received with scepticism at the stables.

Mrs. Warden allowed the poor-law inspector to hand her into the carriage. She asked him to call upon her the following day, and gave him her address.

"To Advocate Abel's!" she cried to the coachman. The fat gentleman lifted his hat with a mealy smile, and the carriage rolled away.

As they gradually left the poor quarter of the town behind, the motion of the carriage became smoother, and the pace increased. And when they emerged upon the broad avenue leading through the villa quarter, the sleek pair snorted with enjoyment of the pure, delicate air from the gardens, and the immovable one indulged, without any sort of necessity, in three masterly cracks of his whip.

Mrs. Warden, too, was conscious of the delight

of finding herself once more in the fresh air. The experiences she had gone through, and, still more, what she had heard from the inspector, had had an almost numbing effect upon her. She began to realize the immeasurable distance between herself and such people as these.

She had often thought there was something quite too sad, nay, almost cruel, in the text: "Many are called, but few are chosen."

Now she understood that it *could* not be otherwise.

How could people so utterly depraved ever attain an elevation at all adequate to the demands of a strict morality? What must be the state of these wretched creatures' consciences? And how should they be able to withstand the manifold temptations of life?

She knew only too well what temptation meant! Was she not incessantly battling against a temptation—perhaps the most perilous of all—the temptation of riches, about which the Scriptures said so many hard things?

She shuddered to think of what would happen if that brutish man and these miserable women suddenly had riches placed in their hands.

Yes, wealth was indeed no slight peril to the soul. It was only yesterday that her husband had tempted her with such a delightful little man-servant—a perfect English groom. But she had resisted the temptation, and answered: "No, Warden, it

would not be right; I will not have a footman on
the box. I dare say we can afford it; but let us beware of overweening luxury. I assure you I don't
require help to get into the carriage and out of it;
I won't even let the coachman get down on my account."

It did her good to think of this now, and her
eyes rested complacently on the empty seat on the
box, beside the immovable one.

Mrs. Abel, who was busy clearing away *Bazars*
and scraps of stuff from the big table, was astonished to see her friend return so soon.

"Why, Emily! Back again already? I've just
been telling the dress-maker that she can go. What
you were saying to me has quite put me out of con-
ceit of my new frock; I can quite well get on without one—" said good-natured Mrs. Abel; but her
lips trembled a little as she spoke.

"Every one must act according to his own conscience," answered Mrs. Warden, quietly, "but I
think it's possible to be too scrupulous."

Mrs. Abel looked up; she had not expected this.

"Just let me tell you what I've gone through,"
said Mrs. Warden, and began her story.

She sketched her first impression of the stuffy
room and the wretched people; then she spoke of
the theft of her purse.

"My husband always declares that people of
that kind can't refrain from stealing," said Mrs.
Abel.

"I'm afraid your husband is nearer the truth than we thought," replied Mrs. Warden.

Then she told about the inspector, and the ingratitude these people had displayed towards the man who cared for them day by day.

But when she came to what she had heard of the poor woman's past life, and still more when she told about the young girl, Mrs. Abel was so overcome that she had to ask the servant to bring some port-wine.

When the girl brought in the tray with the decanter, Mrs. Abel whispered to her: " Tell the dressmaker to wait."

"And then, can you conceive it," Mrs. Warden continued—" I scarcely know how to tell you "— and she whispered.

" What do you say! In one bed! All! Why, it's revolting !" cried Mrs. Abel, clasping her hands.

" Yes, an hour ago I, too, could not have believed it possible," answered Mrs. Warden, " But when you've been on the spot yourself, and seen with your own eyes —"

" Good heavens, Emily, how could you venture into such a place !"

" I am glad I did, and still more glad of the happy chance that brought the inspector on the scene just at the right time. For if it is ennobling to bring succor to the virtuous poor who live clean and frugal lives in their humble sphere, it would be

9

unpardonable to help such people as these to gratify their vile proclivities."

"Yes, you're quite right, Emily! What I can't
understand is how people in a Christian communi-
ty—people who have been baptized and confirmed
—can sink into such a state! Have they not every day—or, at any rate, every Sunday—the opportunity of listening to powerful and impressive ser-
mons? And Bibles, I am told, are to be had for
an incredibly trifling sum."

"Yes, and only to think," added Mrs. Warden,
"that not even the heathen, who are without all
these blessings—that not even they have any excuse for evil-doing; for they have conscience to
guide them."

"And I'm sure conscience speaks clearly enough
to every one who has the will to listen," Mrs. Abel
exclaimed, with emphasis.

"Yes, heaven knows it does," answered Mrs.
Warden, gazing straight before her with a serious
smile.

When the friends parted, they exchanged warm
embraces

Mrs. Warden grasped the ivory handle, entered
the carriage, and drew her train after her. Then
she closed the carriage door—not with a slam, but
slowly and carefully.

"To Madame Labiche's!" she called to the
coachman; then, turning to her friend who had
accompanied her right down to the garden gate,

she said, with a quiet smile : " Now, thank heaven, I can order my silk dress with a good conscience."

"Yes, indeed you can !" exclaimed Mrs. Abel, watching her with tears in her eyes. Then she hastened in-doors.

ROMANCE AND REALITY.

"Just you get married as soon as you can," said Mrs. Olsen.

"Yes, I can't understand why it shouldn't be this very autumn," exclaimed the elder Miss Ludvigsen, who was an enthusiast for ideal love.

"Oh, yes!" cried Miss Louisa, who was certain to be one of the bridesmaids.

"But Sören says he can't afford it," answered the bride elect, somewhat timidly.

"Can't afford it!" repeated Miss Ludvigsen. "To think of a young girl using such an expression! If you're going to let your new-born love be overgrown with prosaic calculations, what will be left of the ideal halo which love alone can cast over life? That a man should be alive to these considerations I can more or less understand—it's in a way his duty; but for a sensitive, womanly heart, in the heyday of sentiment!—No, no, Marie; for heaven's sake, don't let these sordid money-questions darken your happiness."

"Oh, no!" cried Miss Louisa.

"And, besides," Mrs. Olsen chimed in, "your *fiancé* is by no means so badly off. My husband and I began life on much less.—I know you'll say that times were different then. Good heavens, we all know that! What I can't understand is that you don't get tired of telling us so. Don't you think that we old people, who have gone through the transition period, have the best means of comparing the requirements of to-day with those of our youth? You can surely understand that with my experience of house-keeping, I'm not likely to disregard the altered conditions of life; and yet I assure you that the salary your intended receives from my husband, with what he can easily earn by extra work, is quite sufficient to set up house upon."

Mrs. Olsen had become quite eager in her argument, though no one thought of contradicting her. She had so often, in conversations of this sort, been irritated to hear people, and especially young married women, enlarging on the ridiculous cheapness of everything thirty years ago. She felt as though they wanted to make light of the exemplary fashion in which she had conducted her household.

This conversation made a deep impression on the *fiancée*, for she had great confidence in Mrs. Olsen's shrewdness and experience. Since Marie had become engaged to the Sheriff's clerk, the Sheriff's wife had taken a keen interest in her. She was an energetic woman, and, as her own children were already grown up and married, she found

a welcome outlet for her activity in busying herself
with the concerns of the young couple.

Marie's mother, on the other hand, was a very
retiring woman. Her husband, a subordinate gov-
ernment official, had died so early that her pension
was extremely scanty. She came of a good family,
and had learned nothing in her girlhood except to
play the piano. This accomplishment she had long
ceased to practise, and in the course of time had
become exceedingly religious.—

—"Look here, now, my dear fellow, aren't you
thinking of getting married?" asked the Sheriff, in
his genial way.

"Oh yes," answered Sören, with some hesitation, "when I can afford it.

"Afford it!" the Sheriff repeated; "Why, you're
by no means so badly off. I know you have something laid by—"

"A trifle," Sören put in.

"Well, so be it; but it shows, at any rate, that
you have an idea of economy, and that's as good as
money in your pocket. You came out high in your
examination; and, with your family influence and
other advantages at headquarters, you needn't wait
long before applying for some minor appointment;
and once in the way of promotion, you know, you
go ahead in spite of yourself."

Sören bit his pen and looked interested.

"Let us assume," continued his principal, "that,
thanks to your economy, you can set up house with-

out getting into any debt worth speaking of. Then you'll have your salary clear, and whatever you can earn in addition by extra work. It would be strange, indeed, if a man of your ability could not find employment for his leisure time in a rising commercial centre like ours."

Sören reflected all forenoon on what the Sheriff had said. He saw, more and more clearly, that he had over-estimated the financial obstacles to his marriage; and, after all, it was true that he had a good deal of time on his hands out of office hours.

He was engaged to dine with his principal; and his intended, too, was to be there. On the whole, the young people perhaps met quite as often at the Sheriff's as at Marie's home. For the peculiar knack which Mrs. Möller, Marie's mother, had acquired, of giving every conversation a religious turn, was not particularly attractive to them.

There was much talk at table of a lovely little house which Mrs. Olsen had discovered; "A perfect nest for a newly-married couple," as she expressed herself. Sören inquired, in passing, as to the financial conditions, and thought them reasonable enough, if the place answered to his hostess's description.

—Mrs. Olsen's anxiety to see this marriage hurried on was due in the first place, as above hinted, to her desire for mere occupation, and, in the second place, to a vague longing for some event, of

whatever nature, to happen—a psychological phenomenon by no means rare in energetic natures,
living narrow and monotonous lives.

The Sheriff worked in the same direction, partly
in obedience to his wife's orders, and partly because
he thought that Sören's marriage to Marie, who
owed so much to his family, would form another
tie to bind him to the office—for the Sheriff was
pleased with his clerk.

After dinner the young couple strolled about the
garden. They conversed in an odd, short-winded
fashion, until at last Sören, in a tone which was
meant to be careless, threw out the suggestion:
"What should you say to getting married this autumn?"

Marie forgot to express surprise. The same
thought had been running in her own head; so she
answered, looking to the ground: "Well, if you
think you can afford it, I can have no objection."

"Suppose we reckon the thing out," said Sören,
and drew her towards the summer-house.--

Half an hour afterwards they came out, arm-in-
arm, into the sunshine. They, too, seemed to radi-
ate light—the glow of a spirited resolution, formed
after ripe thought and serious counting of the
cost.

Some people might, perhaps, allege that it would
be rash to assume the absolute correctness of a
calculation merely from the fact that two lovers
have arrived at exactly the same total; especially

when the problem happens to bear upon the choice
between renunciation and the supremest bliss.

In the course of the calculation Sören had not
been without misgivings. He remembered how, in
his student days, he had spoken largely of our
duty towards posterity; how he had philosophically
demonstrated the egoistic element in love, and pro-
pounded the ludicrous question whether people had
a right, in pure heedlessness as it were, to bring
children into the world.

But time and practical life had, fortunately, cured
him of all taste for these idle and dangerous mental gymnastics. And, besides, he was far too proper and well-bred to shock his innocent lady-love by
taking into account so indelicate a possibility as
that of their having a large family. Is it not one
of the charms of young love that it should leave
such matters as these to heaven and the stork?*

There was great jubilation at the Sheriff's, and
not there alone. Almost the whole town was thrown
into a sort of fever by the intelligence that the
Sheriff's clerk was to be married in the autumn.
Those who were sure of an invitation to the wedding were already looking forward to it; those who
could not hope to be invited fretted and said spite-
ful things; while those whose case was doubtful
were half crazy with suspense. And all emotions
have their value in a stagnant little town.

* The stork, according to common nursery legends, brings
babies under its wing.

—Mrs. Olsen was a woman of courage; yet her heart beat as she set forth to call upon Mrs. Möller. It is no light matter to ask a mother to let her daughter be married from your house. But she might have spared herself all anxiety.

For Mrs. Möller shrank from every sort of exertion almost as much as she shrank from sin in all its forms. Therefore she was much relieved by Mrs. Olsen's proposition, introduced with a delicacy which did not always characterize that lady's proceedings. However, it was not Mrs. Möller's way to make any show of pleasure or satisfaction. Since everything, in one way or another, was a "cross" to be borne, she did not fail, even in this case, to make it appear that her long-suffering was proof against every trial.

Mrs. Olsen returned home beaming. She would have been balked of half her pleasure in this marriage if she had not been allowed to give the wedding-party; for wedding-parties were Mrs. Olsen's specialty. On such occasions she put her economy aside, and the satisfaction she felt in finding an opening for all her energies made her positively amiable. After all, the Sheriff's post was a good one, and the Olsens had always had a little property besides, which, however, they never talked about.

—So the wedding came off, and a splendid wedding it was. Miss Ludvigsen had written an unrhymed song about true love, which was sung at the feast, and Louisa eclipsed all the other bridesmaids.

The newly-married couple took up their quarters in the nest discovered by Mrs. Olsen, and plunged into that half-conscious existence of festal felicity which the English call the "honeymoon," because it is too sweet; the Germans, "Flitterwochen," because its glory departs so quickly; and we "the wheat-bread days" because we know that there is coarser fare to follow.

But in Sören's cottage the wheat-bread days lasted long; and when heaven sent them a little angel with golden locks, their happiness was as great as we can by any means expect in this weary world.

As for the incomings — well, they were fairly adequate, though Sören had, unfortunately, not succeeded in making a start without getting into debt; but that would, no doubt, come right in time.—

—Yes, in time! The years passed, and with each of them heaven sent Sören a little golden-locked angel. After six years of marriage they had exactly five children. The quiet little town was unchanged, Sören was still the Sheriff's clerk, and the Sheriff's household was as of old; but Sören himself was scarcely to be recognized.

They tell of sorrows and heavy blows of fate which can turn a man's hair gray in a night. Such afflictions had not fallen to Sören's lot. The sorrows that had sprinkled his hair with gray, rounded his shoulders, and made him old before his time, were of a lingering and vulgar type. They were bread-sorrows.

Bread-sorrows are to other sorrows as toothache to other disorders. A simple pain can be conquered in open fight; a nervous fever, or any other " regular " illness, goes through a normal development and comes to a crisis. But while toothache has the long-drawn sameness of the tape-worm, bread-sorrows envelop their victim like a grimy cloud: he puts them on every morning with his threadbare clothes, and he seldom sleeps so deeply as to forget them.

It was in the long fight against encroaching poverty that Sören had worn himself out; and yet he was great at economy.

But there are two sorts of economy: the active and the passive. Passive economy thinks day and night of the way to save a half-penny; active economy broods no less intently on the way to earn a dollar. The first sort of economy, the passive, prevails among us: the active in the great nations —chiefly in America.

Sören's strength lay in the passive direction. He devoted all his spare time and some of his office-hours to thinking out schemes for saving and retrenchment. But whether it was that the luck was against him, or, more probably, that his income was really too small to support a wife and five children –in any case, his financial position went from bad to worse.

Every place in life seems filled to the uttermost, and yet there are people who make their way everywhere. Sören did not belong to this class. He sought in vain for the extra work on which he and Marie had reckoned as a vague but ample source of income. Nor had his good connections availed him aught. There are always plenty of people ready to help young men of promise who can help themselves ; but the needy father of a family is never welcome.

Sören had been a man of many friends. It could not be said that they had drawn back from him, but he seemed somehow to have disappeared from their view. When they happened to meet, there was a certain embarrassment on both sides. Sören no longer cared for the things that interested them, and they were bored when he held forth upon the severity of his daily grind, and the expensiveness of living.

And if, now and then, one of his old friends invited him to a bachelor-party, he did as people are apt to do whose every-day fare is extremely frugal : he ate and drank too much. The lively but well-bred and circumspect Sören declined into a sort of butt, who made rambling speeches, and around whom the young whelps of the party would gather after dinner to make sport for themselves. But what impressed his friends most painfully of all, was his utter neglect of his personal appearance.

For he had once been extremely particular in his dress ; in his student days he had been called " the exquisite Sören." And even after his marriage he

had for some time contrived to wear his modest
attire with a certain air.   But after bitter necessity
had forced him to keep every garment in use an
unnaturally long time, his vanity had at last given
way.   And when once a man's sense of personal
neatness is impaired, he is apt to lose it utterly.
When a new coat became absolutely necessary, it
was his wife that had to awaken him to the fact;
and when his collars became quite too ragged at
the edges, he trimmed them with a pair of scissors.

He had other things to think about, poor fellow.
But when people came into the office, or when he
was entering another person's house, he had a
purely mechanical habit of moistening his fingers
at his lips, and rubbing the lapels of his coat. This
was the sole relic of "the exquisite Sören's" ex-
quisiteness — like one of the rudimentary organs,
dwindled through lack of use, which zoologists find
in certain animals.—

Sören's worst enemy, however, dwelt within him.
In his youth he had dabbled in philosophy, and
this baneful passion for thinking would now attack
him from time to time, crushing all resistance, and,
in the end, turning everything topsy-turvy.

It was when he thought about his children that
this befell him.

When he regarded these little creatures, who, as
he could not conceal from himself, became more
and more neglected as time went on, he found it
impossible to place them under the category of

10

golden-locked angels had sent him by heaven. He
had to admit that heaven does not send us these
gifts without a certain inducement on our side ; and
then Sören asked himself : "Had you any right to
do this?" He thought of his own life, which had
begun under fortunate conditions. His family had
been in easy circumstances ; his father, a govern-
ment official, had given him the best education to
be had in the country ; he had gone forth to the
battle of life fully equipped — and what had come
of it all ?

And how could he equip his children for the
fight into which he was sending them ? They had
begun their life in need and penury, which had, as far
as possible, to be concealed ; they had early learned
the bitter lesson of the disparity between inward
expectations and demands and outward circumstances ; and from their slovenly home they would
take with them the most crushing inheritance, perhaps, under which a man can toil through life : to
wit, poverty with pretensions.

Sören tried to tell himself that heaven would
take care of them. But he was ashamed to do so,
for he felt it was only a phrase of self-excuse, designed to allay the qualms of conscience.

These thoughts were his worst torment : but,
truth to tell, they did not often attack him, for
Sören had sunk into apathy. That was the Sheriff's view of his case. "My clerk was quite a clever
fellow in his time," he used to say. "But, you

know, his hasty marriage, his large family, and all that—in short, he has almost done for himself."

Badly dressed and badly fed, beset with debts and cares, he was worn out and weary before he had accomplished anything. And life went its way, and Sören dragged himself along in its train. He seemed to be forgotten by all save heaven, which, as aforesaid, sent him year by year a little angel with locks of gold—

Sören's young wife had clung faithfully to her husband through these six years, and she, too, had reached the same point.

The first year of her married life had glided away like a dream of dizzy bliss. When she held up the little golden-locked angel for the admiration of her lady friends, she was beautiful with the beauty of perfect maternal happiness; and Miss Ludvigsen said : " Here is love in its ideal form."

But Mrs. Olsen's " nest " soon became too small ; the family increased while the income stood still. She was daily confronted by new claims, new cares, and new duties. Marie set stanchly to work, for she was a courageous and sensible woman.

It is not one of the so-called elevating employments to have charge of a houseful of little children, with no means of satisfying even moderate requirements in respect of comfort and well-being. In addition to this, she was never thoroughly robust ; she oscillated perpetually between having just had, and being just about to have, a child. As she toiled from morning to night, she lost her buoyancy of spirit, and her mind became bitter. She sometimes asked herself: "What is the meaning of it all?"

She saw the eagerness of young girls to be married, and the air of self-complacency with which young men offer to marry them; she thought of her own experience, and felt as though she had been befooled.

But it was not right of Marie to think thus, for she had been excellently brought up.

The view of life to which she had from the first been habituated, was the only beautiful one, the only one that could enable her to preserve her ideals intact. No unlovely and prosaic theory of existence had ever cast its shadow over her development; she knew that love is the most beautiful thing on earth, that it transcends reason and is consummated in marriage; as to children, she had learned to blush when they were mentioned.

A strict watch had always been kept upon her reading. She had read many earnest volumes on the duties of woman; she knew that her happiness lies in being loved by a man, and that her mission is to be his wife. She knew how evil-disposed people will often place obstacles between two lovers, but she knew, too, that true love will at last emerge victorious from the fight. When people met with disaster in the battle of life, it was because they were false to the ideal. She had faith in the ideal, although she did not know what it was.

She knew and loved those poets whom she was allowed to read. Much of their erotics she only half understood, but that made it all the more lovely. She knew that marriage was a serious, a very serious thing, for which a clergyman was indispensable; and she understood that marriages are made in heaven, as engagements are made in the ballroom. But when, in these youthful days, she pictured to herself this serious institution, she seemed to be looking into an enchanted grove, with Cupids weaving garlands, and storks bringing little golden-locked angels under their wings; while before a little cabin in the background, which yet was large enough to contain all the bliss in the world, sat the ideal married couple, gazing into the depths of each other's eyes.

No one had ever been so ill-bred as to say to her: "Excuse me, young lady, would you not like to come with me to a different point of view, and look at the matter from the other side? How if it should turn out to be a mere set-scene of painted pasteboard?"

Sören's young wife had now had ample opportunities of studying the set-scene from the other side.—

Mrs. Olsen had at first come about her early and late, and overwhelmed her with advice and criticism. Both Sören and his wife were many a time heartily tired of her; but they owed the Olsens so much.

Little by little, however, the old lady's zeal cooled

down. When the young people's house was no
longer so clean, so orderly, and so exemplary that
she could plume herself upon her work, she gradually withdrew; and when Sören's wife once in a
while came to ask her for advice or assistance, the
Sheriff's lady would mount her high horse, until
Marie ceased to trouble her. But if, in society,
conversation happened to fall upon the Sheriff's
clerk, and any one expressed compassion for his
poor wife, with her many children and her miserable income, Mrs. Olsen would not fail to put in her
word with great decision: "I can assure you it
would be just the same if Marie had twice as much
to live on and no children at all. You see, she's—"
and Mrs. Olsen made a motion with her hands, as
if she were squandering something abroad, to right
and left.

Marie seldom went to parties, and if she did
appear, in her at least ten-times-altered marriage
dress, it was generally to sit alone in a corner, or
to carry on a tedious conversation with a similarly
situated housewife about the dearness of the times
and the unreasonableness of servant-girls.

And the young ladies who had gathered the gentlemen around them, either in the middle of the
room or wherever they found the most comfortable
chairs to stretch themselves in, whispered to each
other: "How tiresome it is that young married
women can never talk about anything but house-
keeping and the nursery."

In the early days, Marie had often had visits from her many friends. They were enchanted with her charming house, and the little golden-locked angel had positively to be protected from their greedy admiration. But when one of them now chanced to stray in her direction, it was quite a different affair. There was no longer any golden-locked angel to be exhibited in a clean, embroidered frock with red ribbons. The children, who were never presentable without warning, were huddled hastily away—dropping their toys about the floor, forgetting to pick up half-eaten pieces of bread-and-butter from the chairs, and leaving behind them that peculiar atmosphere which one can, at most, endure in one's own children.

Day after day her life dragged on in ceaseless toil. Many a time, when she heard her husband bemoaning the drudgery of his lot, she thought to herself with a sort of defiance : " I wonder which of us two has the harder work ?"

In one respect she was happier than her husband. Philosophy did not enter into her dreams, and when she could steal a quiet moment for reflection, her thoughts were very different from the cogitations of the poor philosopher.

She had no silver plate to polish, no jewelry to take out and deck herself with. But, in the inmost recess of her heart, she treasured all the memories of the first year of her marriage, that year of romantic bliss ; and these memories she would furbish and furbish afresh, till they shone brighter with every year that passed.

But when the weary and despondent housewife, in all secrecy, decked herself out with these jewels of memory, they did not succeed in shedding any brightness over her life in the present. She was scarcely conscious of any connection between the golden-locked angel with the red ribbons and the five-year-old boy who lay grubbing in the dark back yard. These moments snatched her quite away from reality; they were like opium dreams.

Then some one would call for her from an adjoining room, or one of the children would be brought in howling from the street, with a great bump on its forehead. Hastily she would hide away her treasures, resume her customary air of hopeless weariness, and plunge once more into her labyrinth of duties and cares.

—Thus had this marriage fared, and thus did this couple toil onward. They both dragged at the same heavy load; but did they drag in unison? It is sad, but it is true: when the manger is empty, the horses bite each other.—

—There was a great chocolate-party at the Misses Ludvigsen's—all maiden ladies.

"For married women are so prosaic," said the elder Miss Ludvigsen.

"Uh, yes!" cried Louisa.

Every one was in the most vivacious humor, as is generally the case in such company and on such

an occasion ; and, as the gossip went the round of
the town, it arrived in time at Sören's door. All
were agreed that it was a most unhappy marriage,
and a miserable home ; some pitied, others con-
demned.

Then the elder Miss Ludvigsen, with a certain
solemnity, expressed herself as follows : " I can tell
you what was at fault in that marriage, for I know
the circumstances thoroughly. Even before her
marriage there was something calculating, something almost prosaic in Marie's nature, which is entirely foreign to true, ideal love. This fault has
since taken the upperhand, and is avenging itself
cruelly upon both of them. Of course their means
are not great, but what could that matter to two
people who truly loved each other ? for we know
that happiness is not dependent on wealth. Is it
not precisely in the humble home that the omnipo-
tence of love is most beautifully made manifest ?
—And, besides, who can call these two poor ? Has
not heaven richly blessed them with healthy, sturdy
children ? These — these are their true wealth !
And if their hearts had been filled with true, ideal
love, then —then—"

Miss Ludvigsen came to a momentary stand-
still.

" What then ?" asked a courageous young lady.

" Then," continued Miss Ludvigsen, loftily, "then
we should certainly have seen a very different lot
in life assigned to them."

The courageous young lady felt ashamed of herself.

There was a pause, during which Miss Ludvigsen's words sank deep into all hearts. They all felt that this was the truth; any doubt and uneasiness that might perhaps have lurked here and there vanished away. All were confirmed in their steadfast and beautiful faith in true, ideal love; for they were all maiden ladies.

WITHERED LEAVES.

WITHERED LEAVES.

You *may* tire of looking at a single painting, but you *must* tire of looking at many. That is why the eyelids grow so heavy in the great galleries, and the seats are as closely packed as an omnibus on Sunday.

Happy he who has resolution enough to select from the great multitude a small number of pictures, to which he can return every day.

In this way you can appropriate—undetected by the custodians—a little private gallery of your own, distributed through the great halls. Everything which does not belong to this private collection sinks into mere canvas and gilding, a decoration you glance at in passing, but which does not fatigue the eye.

It happens now and then that you discover a picture. hitherto overlooked, which now, after thorough examination, is admitted as one of the select few. The assortment thus steadily increases, and it is even conceivable that by systematically following this method you might make a whole picture-gallery, in this sense, your private property.

But as a rule there is no time for that. You must rapidily take your bearings, putting a cross in the catalogue against the pictures you think of annexing, just as a forester marks his trees as he goes through the wood.

These private collections, as a matter of course, are of many different kinds. One may often search them in vain for the great, recognized masterpieces, while one may find a little, unconsidered picture in the place of honor; and in order to understand the odd arrangement of many of these small collections, one must take as one's cicerone the person whose choice they represent. Here, now, is a picture from a private gallery.—

There hung in a corner of the Salon of 1878 a picture by the English painter Mr. Everton Sainsbury. It made no sensation whatever. It was neither large enough nor small enough to arouse idle curiosity, nor was there a trace of modern extravagance either in composition or in color.

As people passed they gave it a sympathetic glance, for it made a harmonious impression, and the subject was familiar and easily understood.

It represented two lovers who had slightly fallen out, and people smiled as each in his own mind thought of those charming little quarrels which are so vehement and so short, which arise from the most improbable and most varied causes, but invariably end in a kiss.

And yet this picture attracted to itself its own

special public; you could see that it was adopted into several private collections.

As you made your way towards the well-known corner, you would often find the place occupied by a solitary person standing lost in contemplation. At different times, you would come upon all sorts of different people thus absorbed; but they all had the same peculiar expression before that picture, as if it cast a faded, yellowish reflection.

If you approached, the gazer would probably move away; it seemed as though only one person at a time could enjoy that work of art—as though one must be entirely alone with it.—

In a corner of the garden, right against the high wall, stands an open summer-house. It is quite simply built of green lattice-work, which forms a large arch backed by the wall. The whole summer-house is covered with a wild vine, which twines itself from the left side over the arched roof, and droops its slender branches on the right.

It is late autumn. The summer-house has already lost its thick roof of foliage. Only the youngest and most delicate tendrils of the wild vine have any leaves left. Before they fall, departing summer lavishes on them all the color it has left: like light sprays of red and yellow flowers, they hang yet a while to enrich the garden with autumn's melancholy splendor.

The fallen leaves are scattered all around, and right before the summer-house the wind has with

great diligence whirled the loveliest of them together, into a neat little round cairn.

The trees are already leafless, and on a naked
branch sits the little garden-warbler with its rust-
brown breast—like a withered leaf left hanging—
and repeats untiringly a little fragment which it re-
members of its spring-song.

The only thriving thing in the whole picture is
the ivy; for ivy, like sorrow, is fresh both summer
and winter.

It comes creeping along with its soft feelers, it
thrusts itself into the tiniest chinks, it forces its way
through the minutest crannies; and not until it has
waxed wide and strong do we realize that it can no
longer be rooted up, but will inexorably strangle
whatever it has laid its clutches on.

Ivy, however, is like well-bred sorrow; it cloaks
its devastations with fair and glossy leaves. Thus
people wear a glossy mask of smiles, feigning to be
unaware of the ivy-clad ruins among which their lot
is cast.—

In the middle of the open summer-house sits a
young girl on a rush chair; both hands rest in her
lap. She is sitting with bent head and a strange
expression in her beautiful face. It is not vexation
or anger, still less is it commonplace sulkiness, that
utters itself in her features; it is rather bitter and
crushing disappointment. She looks as if she
were on the point of letting something slip away
from her which she has not the strength to hold

fast—as if something were withering between her hands.

The man who is leaning with one hand upon her chair is beginning to understand that the situation is graver than he thought. He has done all he can to get the quarrel, so trivial in its origin, adjusted and forgotten ; he has talked reason, he has tried playfulness; he has besought forgiveness, and humbled himself—perhaps more than he intended —but all in vain. Nothing avails to arouse her out of the listless mood into which she has sunk.

Thus it is with an expression of anxiety that he bends down towards her : " But you know that at heart we love each other so much."

" Then why do we quarrel so easily, and why do we speak so bitterly and unkindly to each other ?"

" Why, my dear ! the whole thing was the merest trifle from the first."

" That's just it ! Do you remember what we said to each other ? How we vied with each other in trying to find the word we knew would be most wounding ? Oh, to think that we used our knowledge of each other's heart to find out the tenderest points, where an unkind word could strike home ! And this we call love !"

" My dear, don't take it so solemnly," he answered, trying a lighter tone. " People may be ever so fond of each other, and yet disagree a little at times ; it can't be otherwise."

" Yes, yes !" she cried. " there must be a love

11

for which discord is impossible, or else—or else I
have been mistaken, and what we call love is nothing but —"

"Have no doubts of love!" he interrupted her,
eagerly; and he depicted in warm and eloquent
words the feeling which ennobles humanity in teach-
ing us to bear with each other's weaknesses; which
confers upon us the highest bliss, since, in spite of
all petty disagreements, it unites us by the fairest
ties.

She had only half listened to him. Her eyes
had wandered over the fading garden, she had in-
haled the heavy atmosphere of dying vegetation—
and she had been thinking of the spring-time, of
hope, of that all-powerful love which was now dying
like an autumn flower.

"Withered leaves," said she, quietly; and rising,
she scattered with her foot all the beautiful leaves
which the wind had taken such pains to heap together.

She went up the avenue leading to the house; he
followed close behind her. He was silent, for he
found not a word to say. A drowsy feeling of
uneasy languor came over him; he asked himself
whether he could overtake her, or whether she were
a hundred miles away.

She walked with her head bent, looking down at
the flower-beds. There stood the asters like torn
paper flowers upon withered potato-shaws; the
dahlias hung their stupid, crinkled heads upon

their broken stems, and the hollyhocks showed small stunted buds at the top, and great wet, rotting flowers clustering down their stalks.

And disappointment and bitterness cut deep into the young heart. As the flowers were dying, she was ripening for the winter of life.

So they disappeared up the avenue. But the empty chair remained standing in the half-withered summer-house, while the wind busied itself afresh in piling up the leaves in a little cairn.

And in the course of time we all come—each in his turn—to seat ourselves on the empty chair in a corner of the garden and gaze on a little cairn of withered leaves.—

THE BATTLE OF WATERLOO.

THE BATTLE OF WATERLOO.

SINCE it is not only entertaining in itself, but also consonant with use and wont, to be in love; and since in our innocent and moral society, one can so much the more safely indulge in these amatory diversions as one runs no risk of being disturbed either by vigilant fathers or pugnacious brothers; and, finally, since one can as easily get out of as get into our peculiarly Norwegian form of betrothal — a half-way house between marriage and free board in a good family — all these things considered, I say, it was not wonderful that Cousin Hans felt profoundly unhappy. For he was not in the least in love.

He had long lived in expectation of being seized by a kind of delirious ecstasy, which, if experienced people are to be trusted, is the infallible symptom of true love. But as nothing of the sort had happened, although he was already in his second year at college, he said to himself: "After all, love is a lottery if you want to win, you must at least table your stake. 'Lend Fortune a helping hand,' as they say in the lottery advertisements."

He looked about him diligently, and closely observed his own heart.

Like a fisher who sits with his line around his forefinger, watching for the least jerk, and wondering when the bite will come, so Cousin Hans held his breath whenever he saw a young lady, wondering whether he was now to feel that peculiar jerk which is well known to be inseparable from true love—that jerk which suddenly makes all the blood rush to the heart, and then sends it just as suddenly up into the head, and makes your face flush red to the very roots of your hair.

But never a bite came. His hair had long ago flushed red to the roots, for Cousin Hans's hair could not be called brown ; but his face remained as pale and as long as ever.

The poor fisherman was growing quite weary, when he one day strolled down to the esplanade. He seated himself on a bench and observed, with a contemptuous air, a squad of soldiers engaged in the invigorating exercise of standing on one leg in the full sunshine, and wriggling their bodies so as to be roasted on both sides.

"Nonsense !"* said Cousin Hans, indignantly ; "it's certainly too dear a joke for a little country like ours to maintain acrobats of that sort. Didn't I see the other day that this so-called army requires 1500 boxes of shoe-blacking, 600 curry-combs,

---

* The English word is used in the original.

3000 yards of gold-lace and 8640 brass buttons?—
It would be better if we saved what we spend in
gold-lace and brass buttons, and devoted our half-
pence to popular enlightenment," said Cousin Hans.

For he was infected by the modern ideas, which
are unfortunately beginning to make way among us,
and which will infallibly end in overthrowing the
whole existing fabric of society.

"Good-bye, then, for the present," said a lady's
voice close behind him.

"Good-bye for the present, my dear," answered a
deep, masculine voice.

Cousin Hans turned slowly, for it was a warm
day.   He discovered a military-looking old man in a
close-buttoned black coat, with an order at his button-hole, a neck-cloth twisted an incredible number
of times around his throat, a well-brushed hat, and
light trousers.   The gentleman nodded to a young
lady, who went off towards the town, and then continued his walk along the ramparts.

Weary of waiting as he was, Cousin Hans could
not help following the young girl with his eyes as
she hastened away.   She was small and trim, and
he observed with interest that she was one of the
few women who do not make a little inward turn
with the left foot as they lift it from the ground.

This was a great merit in the young man's eyes;
for Cousin Hans was one of those sensitive, ob-
servant natures who are alone fitted really to appreciate a woman at her full value.

After a few steps the lady turned, no doubt in order to nod once again to the old officer; but by the merest chance her eyes met those of Cousin Hans.

At last occurred what he had so long been expecting: he felt the bite! His blood rushed about just in the proper way, he lost his breath, his head became hot, a cold shiver ran down his back, and he grew moist between the fingers. In short, all the symptoms supervened which, according to the testimony of poets and experienced prose-writers, betoken real, true, genuine love.

There was, indeed, no time to be lost. He hastily snatched up his gloves, his stick, and his student's cap, which he had laid upon the bench, and set off after the lady across the esplanade and towards the town.

In the great, corrupt communities abroad this sort of thing is not allowable. There the conditions of life are so impure that a well-bred young man would never think of following a reputable woman. And the few reputable women there are in those nations, would be much discomposed to find themselves followed.

But in our pure and moral atmosphere we can, fortunately, permit our young people somewhat greater latitude, just on account of the strict propriety of our habits.

Cousin Hans, therefore, did not hesitate a moment in obeying the voice of his heart; and the

young lady, who soon observed what havoc she
had made with the glance designed for the old
soldier, felt the situation piquant and not unpleasing.

The passers-by, who, of course, at once saw what
was going on (be it observed that this is one of the
few scenes of life in which the leading actors are
quite unconscious of their audience), thought, for
the most part, that the comedy was amusing to
witness. They looked round and smiled to themselves; for they all knew that either it would lead
to nothing, in which case it was only the most innocent of youthful amusements; or it would lead
to an engagement, and an engagement is the most
delightful thing in the world.

While they thus pursued their course at a fitting
distance, now on the same sidewalk and now on
opposite sides of the street, Cousin Hans had ample time for reflection.

As to the fact of his being in love he was quite
clear. The symptoms were all there; he knew
that he was in for it, in for real, true, genuine, love;
and he was happy in the knowledge. Yes, so happy was Cousin Hans that he, who at other times
was apt to stand upon his rights, accepted with a
quiet, complacent smile all the jostlings and shoves,
the smothered objurgations and other unpleasant-
nesses, which inevitably befall any one who rushes
hastily along a crowded street, keeping his eyes
fixed upon an object in front of him.

No — the love was obvious, indubitable. That settled, he tried to picture to himself the beloved one's, the heavenly creature's, mundane circumstances. And there was no great difficulty in that; she had been walking with her old father, had suddenly discovered that it was past twelve o'clock, and had hastily said good-bye for the present, in order to go home and see to the dinner. For she was doubtless domestic, this sweet creature, and evidently motherless.

The last conjecture was, perhaps, a result of the dread of mothers-in-law inculcated by all reputable authors; but it was none the less confident on that account. And now it only remained for Cousin Hans to discover, in the first place, where she lived, in the second place who she was, and in the third place how he could make her acquaintance.

Where she lived he would soon learn, for was she not on her way home? Who she was, he could easily find out from the neighbors. And as for making her acquaintance — good heavens! is not a little difficulty an indispensable part of a genuine romance?

Just as the chase was at its height, the quarry disappeared into a gate-way; and it was really high time, for, truth to tell, the hunter was rather exhausted.

He read with a certain relief the number, "34," over the gate, then went a few steps farther on, in order to throw any possible observer off the scent, and stopped beside a street-lamp to recover his breath. It was, as aforesaid, a warm day; and this, combined with his violent emotion, had thrown Hans into a strong perspiration. His toilet, too, had been disarranged by the reckless eagerness with which he had hurled himself into the chase.

He could not help smiling at himself, as he stood and wiped his face and neck, adjusted his necktie, and felt his collar, which had melted on the sunny side. But it was a blissful smile; he was in that frame of mind in which one sees, or at any rate apprehends, nothing of the external world; and he said to himself, half aloud, "Love endures everything, accepts everything."

"And perspires freely," said a fat little gentleman whose white waistcoat suddenly came within Cousin Hans's range of vision.

"Oh, is that you, uncle?" he said, a little abashed.

"Of course it is," answered Uncle Frederick. "I've left the shady side of the street expressly to save you from being roasted. Come along with me."

Thereupon he tried to drag his nephew with him, but Hans resisted. "Do you know who lives at No. 34, uncle?"

"Not in the least; but do let us get into the shade," said Uncle Frederick; for there were two things he could not endure: heat and laughter—the first on account of his corpulence, and the second on account of what he himself called "his apoplectic tendencies."

"By-the-bye," he said, when they reached the cool side of the street, and he had taken his nephew by the arm, "now that I think of it, I do know, quite well, who lives in No. 34; it's old Captain Schrappe."

"Do you know him?" asked Cousin Hans, anxiously.

"Yes, a little, just as half the town knows him, from having seen him on the esplanade, where he walks every day."

"Yes, that was just where I saw him," said his nephew. "What an interesting old gentleman he looks. I should like so much to have a talk with him."

"That wish you can easily gratify," answered Uncle Frederick. "You need only place yourself anywhere on the ramparts and begin drawing lines in the sand, then he'll come to you."

"Come to you?" said Cousin Hans.

"Yes, he'll come and talk to you. But you must be careful: he's dangerous."

"Eh?" said Cousin Hans.

"He was once very nearly the end of me."

"Ah!" said Cousin Hans.

"Yes, with his talk, you understand."

"Oh?" said Cousin Hans.

"You see, he has two stories," continued Uncle Frederick, "the one, about a sham fight in Sweden, is a good half-hour long. But the other, the battle of Waterloo, generally lasts from an hour and a

half to two hours. I have heard it three times."
And Uncle Frederick sighed deeply.

"Are they so very tedious, then, these stories?"
asked Cousin Hans.

"Oh, they're well enough for once in a way," answered his uncle, "and if you should get into conversation with the captain, mark what I tell you:
If you get off with the short story, the Swedish one,
you have nothing to do but alternately to nod and
shake your head. You'll soon pick up the lay of
the land."

"The lay of the land?" said Cousin Hans.

"Yes, you must know that he draws the whole
manœuvre for you in the sand; but it's easy enough
to understand if only you keep your eye on A and
B. There's only one point where you must be
careful not to put your foot in it." .

"Does he get impatient, then, if you don't understand?" asked Cousin Hans.

"No, quite the contrary; but if you show that
you're not following, he begins at the beginning
again, you see! The crucial point in the sham
fight," continued his uncle, "is the movement made
by the captain himself, in spite of the general's
orders, which equally embarrassed both friends and
foes. It was this stroke of genius, between ourselves, which forced them to give him the Order
of the Sword, to induce him to retire. So when
you come to this point, you must nod violent-
ly, and say: 'Of course — the only reasonable move

—the key to the position.' Remember that—the key."

"The key," repeated Cousin Hans.

"But," said his uncle, looking at him with anticipatory compassion, "if, in your youthful love of adventure, you should bring on yourself the long story, the one about Waterloo, you must either keep quite silent or have all your wits about you. I once had to swallow the whole description over again, only because, in my eagerness to show how thoroughly I understood the situation, I happened to move Kellermann's dragoons instead of Milhaud's cuirassiers!"

"What do you mean by moving the dragoons, uncle?" asked Cousin Hans.

"Oh, you'll understand well enough, if you come in for the long one. But," added Uncle Frederick, in a solemn tone, "beware, I warn you, beware of Blücher!"

"Blücher?" said Cousin Hans.

"I won't say anything more. But what makes you wish to know about this old original? What on earth do you want with him."

"Does he walk there every forenoon?" asked Hans.

"Every forenoon, from eleven to one, and every afternoon, from five to seven. But what interest—?"

"Has he many children?" interrupted Hans.

"Only one daughter; but what the deuce—?"

"Good - bye, uncle!" I must get home to my books."

"Stop a bit! Aren't you going to Aunt Maren's this evening? She asked me to invite you."

"No, thanks, I haven't time," shouted Cousin Hans, who was already several paces away.

"There's to be a ladies' party—young ladies!" bawled Uncle Frederick; for he did not know what had come over his nephew.

But Hans shook his head with a peculiar energetic contempt, and disappeared round the corner.

"The deuce is in it," thought Uncle Frederick, "the boy is crazy, or—oh, I have it!—he's in love! He was standing here, babbling about love, when I found him—outside No. 34. And then his interest in old Schrappe! Can he be in love with Miss Betty? Oh, no," thought Uncle Frederick, shaking his head, as he, too, continued on his way, "I don't believe he has sense enough for that."

II.

Cousin Hans did not eat much dinner that day. People in love never eat much, and, besides, he did not care for rissoles.

At last five o'clock struck. He had already taken up his position on the ramparts, whence he could survey the whole esplanade. Quite right:

12

there came the black frock-coat, the light trousers, and the well-brushed hat.

Cousin Hans felt his heart palpitate a little. At first he attributed this to a sense of shame in thus craftily setting a trap for the good old captain. But he soon discovered that it was the sight of the beloved one's father that set his blood in a ferment. Thus reassured, he began, in accordance with Uncle Frederick's advice, to draw strokes and angles in the sand, attentively fixing his eyes, from time to time, upon the Castle of Akerhuus.

The whole esplanade was quiet and deserted. Cousin Hans could hear the captain's firm steps approaching; they came right up to him and stopped. Hans did not look up; the captain advanced two more paces and coughed. Hans drew a long and profoundly significant stroke with his stick, and then the old fellow could contain himself no longer.

"Aha, young gentleman," he said, in a friendly tone, taking off his hat, "are you making a plan of our fortifications?"

Cousin Hans assumed the look of one who is awakened from deep contemplation, and, bowing politely, he answered with some embarrassment: "No, it's only a sort of habit I have of trying to take my bearings wherever I may be."

"An excellent habit, a most excellent habit," the captain exclaimed with warmth.

"It strengthens the memory," Cousin Hans remarked, modestly.

"Certainly, certainly, sir!" answered the captain, who was beginning to be much pleased by this modest young man.

"Especially in situations of any complexity," continued the modest young man, rubbing out his strokes with his foot.

"Just what I was going to say!" exclaimed the captain, delighted. "And, as you may well believe, drawings and plans are especially indispensable in military science. Look at a battle-field, for example."

"Ah, battles are altogether too intricate for me," Cousin Hans interrupted, with a smile of humility.

"Don't say that, sir!" answered the kindly old man. "When once you have a bird's-eye view of the ground and of the positions of the armies, even a tolerably complicated battle can be made quite comprehensible.—This sand, now, that we have before us here, could very well be made to give us an idea, in miniature, of, for example, the battle of Waterloo."

"I have come in for the long one," thought Cousin Hans, "but never mind!* I love her."

"Be so good as to take a seat on the bench here," continued the captain, whose heart was rejoiced at the thought of so intelligent a hearer, "and I shall try to give you in short outline a picture of that momentous and remarkable battle—if it interests you?"

"Many thanks, sir," answered Cousin Hans,

* In English in the original.

"nothing could interest me more. But I'm afraid
you'll find it terribly hard work to make it clear to
a poor, ignorant civilian."

"By no means; the whole thing is quite simple
and easy, if only you are first familiar with the lay
of the land," the amiable old gentleman assured
him, as he took his seat at Hans's side, and cast
an inquiring glance around.

While they were thus seated, Cousin Hans examined the captain more closely, and he could not
but admit that in spite of his sixty years, Captain
Schrappe was still a handsome man. He wore his
short, iron-gray mustaches a little turned up at the
ends, which gave him a certain air of youthfulness.
On the whole, he bore a strong resemblance to
King Oscar the First on the old sixpenny-pieces.

And as the captain rose and began his disserta-
tion, Cousin Hans decided in his own mind that he
had every reason to be satisfied with his future
father-in-law's exterior.

The captain took up a position in a corner of
the ramparts, a few paces from the bench, whence
he could point all around him with a stick. Cousin
Hans followed what he said, closely, and took all
possible trouble to ingratiate himself with his future
father-in-law.

"We will suppose, then, that I am standing here
at the farm of Belle-Alliance, where the Emperor
has his headquarters; and to the north fourteen
miles from Waterloo—we have Brussels, that is to

say, just about at the corner of the gymnastic-
school.

"The road there along the rampart is the highway leading to Brussels, and here," the captain
rushed over the plain of Waterloo, "here in the
grass we have the Forest of Soignies. On the
highway to Brussels, and in front of the forest, the
English are stationed—you must imagine the north-
ern part of the battle-field somewhat higher than it
is here. On Wellington's left wing, that is to say,
to the eastward—here in the grass—we have the
Château of Hougoumont; that must be marked,"
said the captain, looking about him.

The serviceable Cousin Hans at once found a
stick, which was fixed in the ground at this important point.

"Excellent!" cried the captain, who saw that he
had found an interested and imaginative listener.
"You see it's from this side that we have to expect the Prussians."

Cousin Hans noticed that the captain picked up
a stone and placed it in the grass with an air of
mystery.

"Here at Hougoumont," the old man continued, "the battle began. It was Jerome who made
the first attack. He took the wood; but the château held out, garrisoned by Wellington's best
troops.

"In the mean time Napoleon, here at Belle-Alliance, was on the point of giving Marshal Ney or-

ders to commence the main attack upon Wellington's centre, when he observed a column of troops
approaching from the east, behind the bench, over
there by tree."

Cousin Hans looked round, and began to feel
uneasy: could Blücher be here already?

"Blü—Blü—" he murmured, tentatively,

"It was Bülow," the captain fortunately went
on, "who approached with thirty thousand Prussians. Napoleon made his arrangements hastily
to meet this new enemy, never doubting that
Grouchy, at any rate, was following close on the
Prussians' heels.

"You see, the Emperor had on the previous day
detached Marshal Grouchy with the whole right
wing of the army, about fifty thousand men, to
hold Blücher and Bülow in check. But Grouchy
—but of course all this is familiar to you—" the
captain broke off.

Cousin Hans nodded reassuringly.

"Ney, accordingly, began the attack with his
usual intrepidity. But the English cavalry hurled
themselves upon the Frenchmen, broke their ranks,
and forced them back with the loss of two eagles
and several cannons. Milhaud rushes to the rescue
with his cuirassiers, and the Emperor himself, seeing the danger, puts spurs to his horse and gallops
down the incline of Belle-Alliance."

Away rushed the captain, prancing like a horse,
in his eagerness to show how the Emperor rode

through thick and thin, rallied Ney's troops, and sent them forward to a fresh attack.

Whether it was that there lurked a bit of the poet in Cousin Hans, or that the captain's representation was really very vivid, or that—and this is probably the true explanation—he was in love with the captain's daughter, certain it is that Cousin Hans was quite carried away by the situation.

He no longer saw a queer old captain prancing sideways, he saw, through the cloud of smoke, the Emperor himself on his white horse with the black eyes, as we know it from the engravings. He tore away over hedge and ditch, over meadow and garden, his staff with difficulty keeping up with him. Cool and calm, he sat firmly in his saddle, with his half-unbuttoned gray coat, his white breeches, and his little hat, crosswise on his head. His face expressed neither weariness nor anxiety; smooth and pale as marble, it gave to the whole figure in the simple uniform on the white horse an exalted, almost a spectral, aspect.

Thus he swept on his course, this sanguinary little monster, who in three days had fought three battles. All hastened to clear the way for him, flying peasants, troops in reserve or advancing—aye, even the wounded and dying dragged themselves aside, and looked up at him with a mixture of terror and admiration, as he tore past them like a cold thunderbolt.

Scarcely had he shown himself among the sol-

diers before they all fell into order as though by
magic, and a moment afterwards the undaunted
Ney could once more vault into the saddle to re-
new the attack.   And this time he bore down the
English and established himself in the farm-house
of La Haie-Sainte.

Napoleon is once more at Belle-Alliance.

"And now here comes Bülow from the east—under
the bench here, you see—and the Emperor sends
General Mouton to meet him.   At half-past four
(the battle had begun at one o'clock) Wellington
attempts to drive Ney out of La Haie-Sainte.   But
Ney, who now saw that everything depended on
obtaining possession of the ground in front of the
wood—the sand here by the border of the grass,"
the captain threw his glove over to the spot indi-
cated, " Ney, you see, calls up the reserve brigade
of Milhaud's cuirassiers and hurls himself at the
enemy.

" Presently his men were seen upon the heights,
and already the people around the Emperor were
shouting ' Victoire !'

" ' It is an hour too late,' answered Napoleon.

" As he now saw that the Marshal in his new position was suffering much from the enemy's fire,
he determined to go to his assistance, and, at the
same time, to try to crush Wellington at one blow.
He chose for the execution of this plan, Kellermann's famous dragoons and the heavy cavalry of
the guard.   Now comes one of the crucial moments

of the fight; you must come out here upon the battle-field!"

Cousin Hans at once rose from the bench and took the position the captain pointed out to him.

"Now you are Wellington!" Cousin Hans drew himself up. "You are standing there on the plain with the greater part of the English infantry. Here comes the whole of the French cavalry rushing down upon you. Milhaud has joined Kellermann; they form an illimitable multitude of horses, breast-plates, plumes and shining weapons. Surround yourself with a square!"

Cousin Hans stood for a moment bewildered; but presently he understood the captain's meaning. He hastily drew a square of deep strokes around him in the sand.

"Right!" cried the captain, beaming, "Now the Frenchmen cut into the square; the ranks break, but join again, the cavalry wheels away and gathers for a fresh attack. Wellington has at every moment to surround himself with a new square.

"The French cavalry fight like lions: the proud memories of the Emperor's campaigns fill them with that confidence of victory which made his armies invincible. They fight for victory, for glory, for the French eagles, and for the little cold man who, they know, stands on the height behind them; whose eye follows every single man, who sees all, and forgets nothing.

"But to-day they have an enemy who is not easy

to deal with. They stand where they stand, these Englishmen, and if they are forced a step backwards, they regain their position the next moment. They have no eagles and no Emperor; when they fight they think neither of military glory nor of revenge; but they think of home. The thought of never seeing again the oak-trees of Old England is the most melancholy an Englishman knows. Ah, no, there is one which is still worse : that of coming home dishonored. And when they think that the proud fleet, which they know is lying to the northward waiting for them, would deny them the honor of a salute, and that Old England would not recognize her sons—then they grip their muskets tighter, they forget their wounds and their flowing blood; silent and grim, they clinch their teeth, and hold their post, and die like men."

Twenty times were the squares broken and reformed, and twelve thousand brave Englishmen fell. Cousin Hans could understand how Wellington wept, when he said, "Night or Blücher!"

The captain had in the mean time left Belle-Alliance, and was spying around in the grass behind the bench, while he continued his exposition which grew more and more vivid: "Wellington was now in reality beaten and a total defeat was inevitable," cried the captain, in a sombre voice, "when this fellow appeared on the scene!" And as he said this, he kicked the stone which Cousin Hans had seen him concealing, so that it rolled in upon the field of battle.

"Now or never," thought Cousin Hans.

"Blücher!" he cried.

"Exactly!" answered the captain, "it's the old werewolf Blücher, who comes marching upon the field with his Prussians."

So Grouchy never came; there was Napoleon, deprived of his whole right wing, and facing 150,000 men. But with never-failing coolness he gives his orders for a great change of front.

But it was too late, and the odds were too vast.

Wellington, who, by Blücher's arrival, was enabled to bring his reserve into play, now ordered his whole army to advance. And yet once more the Allies were forced to pause for a moment by a furious charge led by Ney—the lion of the day.

"Do you see him there!" cried the captain, his eyes flashing.

And Cousin Hans saw him, the romantic hero, Duke of Elchingen, Prince of Moskwa, son of a cooper in Saarlouis, Marshal and Peer of France. He saw him rush onward at the head of his battalions—five horses had been shot under him—with his sword in his hand, his uniform torn to shreds, hatless, and with the blood streaming down his face.

And the battalions rallied and swept ahead; they followed their Prince of Moskwa, their savior at the Beresina, into the hopeless struggle for the Emperor and for France. Little did they dream that, six months later, the King of France would have their dear prince shot as a traitor to his country in the gardens of the Luxembourg.

There he rushed around, rallying and directing his troops, until there was nothing more for the general to do; then he plied his sword like a common soldier until all was over, and he was carried away in the rout. For the French army fled.

The Emperor threw himself into the throng; but the terrible hubbub drowned his voice, and in the twilight no one knew the little man on the white horse.

Then he took his stand in a little square of his Old Guard, which still held out upon the plain; he would fain have ended his life on his last battle-field. But his generals flocked around him, and the old grenadiers shouted: "Withdraw, Sire! Death will not have you."

They did not know that it was because the *Emperor* had forfeited his right to die as a French soldier. They led him half-resisting from the field; and, unknown in his own army, he rode away into the darkness of the night, having lost everything. "So ended the battle of Waterloo," said the captain, as he seated himself on the bench and arranged his neck-cloth.

—Cousin Hans thought with indignation of Uncle Frederick, who had spoken of Captain Schrappe in such a tone of superiority. He was, at least, a far more interesting personage than an old official mill-horse like Uncle Frederick.

Hans now went about and gathered up the gloves and other small objects which the generals, in the heat of the fight, had scattered over the battle-field to mark the positions; and, as he did so, he stumbled upon old Blücher. He picked him up and examined him carefully.

He was a hard lump of granite, knubbly as sugar-candy, which almost seemed to bear a personal resemblance to "Feldtmarschall Vorwärts." Hans turned to the captain with a polite bow.

"Will you allow me, captain, to keep this stone. It will be the best possible memento of this interesting and instructive conversation, for which I am really most grateful to you." And thereupon he put Blücher into his coat-tail pocket.

The captain assured him that it had been a real pleasure to him to observe the interest with which his young friend had followed the exposition. And this was nothing but the truth, for he was positively enraptured with Cousin Hans.

"Come and sit down now, young man. We deserve a little rest after a ten-hours' battle," he added, smiling.

Cousin Hans seated himself on the bench and felt his collar with some anxiety. Before coming out, he had put on the most fascinating one his wardrobe afforded. Fortunately, it had retained its stiffness; but he felt the force of Wellington's words: "Night or Blücher"—for it would not have held out much longer.

It was fortunate, too, that the warm afternoon
sun had kept strollers away from the esplanade.
Otherwise a considerable audience would probably
have gathered around these two gentlemen, who
went on gesticulating with their arms, and now and
then prancing around.

They had had only one on-looker — the sentry
who stands at the corner of the gymnastic-school.

His curiosity had enticed him much too far from
his post, for he had marched several leagues along
the highway from Brussels to Waterloo. The captain would certainly have called him to order long
ago for this dereliction of duty but for the fact that
the inquisitive private had been of great strategic
importance. He represented, as he stood there,
the whole of Wellington's reserve ; and now that
the battle was over the reserve retired in good order northward towards Brussels, and again took up
le poste perdu at the corner of the gymnastic-school.

III.

" Suppose you come home and have some supper with me," said the captain ; " my house is very
quiet, but I think perhaps a young man of your
character may have no great objection to passing
an evening in a quiet family."

Cousin Hans's heart leaped high with joy : he

accepted the invitation in the modest manner peculiar to him, and they were soon on the way to
No. 34.

How curiously fortune favored him to-day ! Not
many hours had passed since he saw her for the
first time ; and now, in the character of a special
favorite of her father, he was hastening to pass the
evening in her company.

The nearer they approached to No. 34, in the
more life-like colors did the enchanting vision of
Miss Schrappe stand before his eyes ; the blonde
hair curling over the forehead, the lithe figure, and
then these roguish, light-blue eyes !

His heart beat so that he could scarcely speak,
and as they mounted the stair he had to take firm
hold of the railing ; his happiness made him almost
dizzy.

In the parlor, a large corner-room, they found no
one. The captain went out to summon his daughter, and Hans heard him calling, " Betty !"

Betty ! What a lovely name, and how well it
suited that lovely being !

The happy lover was already thinking how delightful it would be when he came home from his
work at dinner-time, and could call out into the
kitchen : " Betty ! is dinner ready ?"

At this moment the captain entered the room
again with his daughter. She came straight up to
Cousin Hans, took his hand, and bade him welcome.

But she added, " You must really excuse me de-

serting you again at once, for I am in the middle of
a dish of buttered eggs, and that's no joke, I can
tell you."

Thereupon she disappeared again; the captain
also withdrew to prepare for the meal, and Cousin
Hans was once more alone.

The whole meeting had not lasted many seconds,
and yet it seemed to Cousin Hans that in these
moments he had toppled from ledge to ledge, many
fathoms down, into a deep, black pit. He supported
himself with both hands against an old, high-backed
easy-chair; he neither heard, saw, nor thought; but
half mechanically he repeated to himself: " It was
not she—it was not she !"

No, it was not she. The lady whom he had just
seen, and who must consequently be Miss Schrappe,
had not a trace of blonde hair curling over her brow.
On the contrary, she had dark hair, smoothed down
to both sides Her eyes were not in the least roguish or light blue, but serious and dark-gray—in
short, she was as unlike the charmer as possible.

After his first paralysis, Cousin Hans's blood began to boil; a violent anguish seized him : he raged
against the captain, against Miss Schrappe. against
Uncle Frederick and Wellington, and the whole
world.

He would smash the big mirror and all the furni-
ture, and then jump out of the corner window; or
he would take his hat and stick, rush down-stairs,
leave the house, and never more set foot in it ; or

he would at least remain no longer than was absolutely necessary.

Little by little he became calmer, but a deep melancholy descended upon him. He had felt the unspeakable agony of disappointment in his first love, and when his eye fell on his own image in the mirror, he shook his head compassionately.

The captain now returned, well-brushed and spick and span. He opened a conversation about the politics of the day. It was with difficulty that Cousin Hans could even give short and commonplace answers; it seemed as though all that had interested him in Captain Schrappe had entirely evaporated. And now Hans remembered that on the way home from the esplanade he had promised to give him the whole sham fight in Sweden after supper.

"Will you come, please; supper is ready," said Miss Betty, opening the door into the dining-room, which was lighted with candles.

Cousin Hans could not help eating, for he was hungry; but he looked down at his plate and spoke little.

Thus the conversation was at first confined for the most part to the father and daughter. The captain, who thought that this bashful young man was embarrassed by Miss Betty's presence, wanted to give him time to collect himself.

"How is it you haven't invited Miss Beck this evening, since she's leaving town to-morrow," said

13

the old man. "You two could have entertained our guest with some duets."

"I asked her to stay, when she was here this afternoon; but she was engaged to a farewell party with some other people she knows."

Cousin Hans pricked up his ears; could this be the lady of the morning that they were speaking about?

"I told you she came down to the esplanade to say good-bye to me," continued the captain. "Poor girl! I'm really sorry for her."

There could no longer be any doubt.

"I beg your pardon—are you speaking of a lady with curly hair and large blue eyes?" asked Cousin Hans.

"Exactly," answered the captain, "do you know Miss Beck?"

"No," answered Hans, "it only occurred to me that it might be a lady I met down on the esplanade about twelve o'clock."

"No doubt it was she" said the captain. "A pretty girl, isn't she?"

"I thought her beautiful," answered Hans, with conviction. "Has she had any trouble?—I thought I heard you say"—

"Well, yes; you see she was engaged for some months"—

"Nine weeks," interrupted Miss Betty.

"Indeed! was that all? At any rate her *fiancé* has just broken off the engagement, and that's why

she is going away for a little while—very naturally
—to some relations in the west-country, I think."

So she had been engaged—only for nine weeks,
indeed—but still, it was a little disappointing.
However, Cousin Hans understood human nature,
and he had seen enough of her that morning to
know that her feelings towards her recreant lover
could not have been true love.   So he said:

" If it's the lady I saw to-day, she seemed to take
the matter pretty lightly."

" That's just what I blame her for," answered
Miss Betty.

" Why so?" answered Cousin Hans, a little sharp-
ly: for, on the whole, he did not like the way in
which the young lady made her remarks.   " Would
you have had her mope and pine away?"

" No, not at all," answered Miss Schrappe ; " but,
in my opinion, it would have shown more strength
of character if she had felt more indignant at her
fiancé's conduct."   ·

" I should say, on the contrary, that it shows most
admirable strength of character that she should
bear no ill-will and feel no anger; for a woman's
strength lies in forgiveness," said Cousin Hans, who
grew eloquent in defence of his lady-love.

Miss Betty thought that if people in general
would show more indignation when an engagement
was broken off, as so often happened, perhaps
young people would be more cautious in these
matters.

Cousin Hans, on the other hand, was of opinion that when a *fiancé* discovered, or even suspected, that he had made a mistake, and that what he had taken for love was not the real, true, and genuine article, he was not only bound to break off the engagement with all possible speed, but it was the positive duty of the other party, and of all friends and acquaintances, to excuse and forgive him, and to say as little as possible about the matter, in order that it might the sooner be forgotten.

Miss Betty answered hastily that she did not think it at all the right thing that young people should enter into experimental engagements while they keep a look out for true love.

This remark greatly irritated Cousin Hans, but he had no time to reply, for at that moment the captain rose from the table.

There was something about Miss Schrappe that he really could not endure; and he was so much absorbed in this thought that, for a time, he almost forgot the melancholy intelligence that the beloved one—Miss Beck—was leaving town to-morrow

He could not but admit that the captain's daughter was pretty, very pretty; she seemed to be both domestic and sensible, and it was clear that she devoted herself to her old father with touching tenderness. And yet Cousin Hans said to himself: " Poor thing, who would want to marry her?"

For she was entirely devoid of that charming helplessness which is so attractive in a young girl;

when she spoke, it was with an almost odious repose and decision.   She never came in with any of
those fascinating half-finished sentences, such as
"Oh, I don't know if you understand me—there
are so few people that understand me—I don't
know how to express what I mean ; but I feel it so
strongly."   In short, there was about Miss Schrappe
nothing of that vagueness and mystery which is
woman's most exquisite charm.

Furthermore, he had a suspicion that she was
"learned."   And every one, surely, must agree with
Cousin Hans that if a woman is to fulfil her mission in this life (that is to say, to be a man's wife)
she ought clearly to have no other acquirements
than those her husband wishes her to have, or himself confers upon her.   Any other fund of knowledge must always be a dowry of exceedingly doubtful value.

Cousin Hans was in the most miserable of moods.
It was only eight o'clock, and he did not think it
would do to take his departure before half-past nine.
The captain had already settled himself at the table, prepared to begin the sham-fight.   There was no
chance of escape, and Hans took a seat at his side.

Opposite to him sat Miss Betty, with her sewing,
and with a book in front of her.   He leaned forward and discovered that it was a German novel
of the modern school.

It was precisely one of those works which Hans
was wont to praise loudly when he developed his

advanced views, colored with a little dash of free-thought. But to find this book here, in a lady's hands, and, what was more, in German (Hans had read it in a translation), was in the last degree unpleasing to him.

Accordingly, when Miss Betty asked if he liked the novel, he answered that it was one of the books which should only be read by men of ripened judgment and established principles, and that it was not at all suited for ladies.

He saw that the girl flushed, and he felt that he had been rude. But he was really feeling desperate, and, besides, there was something positively irritating in this superior little person.

He was intensely worried and bored ; and, to fulfil the measure of his suffering, the captain began to make Battalion B advance " under cover of the night."

Cousin Hans now watched the captain moving match-boxes, penknives, and other small objects about the table. He nodded now and then, but he did not pay the slightest attention. He thought of the lovely Miss Beck, whom he was, perhaps, never to see again ; and now and then he stole a glance at Miss Schrappe, to whom he had been so rude.

He gave a sudden start as the captain slapped him on the shoulder, with the words, "And it was this point that I was to occupy. What do you think of that ?"

Uncle Frederick's words flashed across Cousin Hans's mind, and, nodding vehemently, he said: "Of course, the only thing to be done—the key to the position?"

The captain started back and became quite serious. But when he saw Cousin Hans's disconcerted expression, his good-nature got the upperhand, and he laughed and said:

"No, my dear sir! there you're quite mistaken. However," he added, with a quiet smile, "it's a mistake which you share with several of our highest military authorities. No, now let me show you the key to the position."

And then he began to demonstrate at large that the point which he had been ordered to occupy was quite without strategical importance; while, on the other hand, the movement which he made on his own responsibility placed the enemy in the direst embarrassment, and would have delayed the advance of Corps B by several hours.

Tired and dazed as Cousin Hans was, he could not help admiring the judicious course adopted by the military authorities towards Captain Schrappe, if, indeed, there was anything in Uncle Frederick's story about the Order of the Sword.

For if the captain's original manœuvre was, strategically speaking, a stroke of genius, it was undoubtedly right that he should receive a decoration. But, on the other hand, it was no less clear that the man who could suppose that in a sham-

fight it was in the least desirable to delay or embar-
rass any one was quite out of place in an army like
ours.   He ought to have known that the true object of the manœuvres was to let the opposing
armies, with their baggage and commissariat wag-
ons, meet at a given time and in a given place, there
to have a general picnic.

While Hans was buried in these thoughts, the captain finished the sham-fight.   He was by no means
so pleased with his listener as he had been upon
the esplanade ; he seemed, somehow, to have become absent-minded.

It was now nine o'clock ; but, as Cousin Hans
had made up his mind that he would hold out till
half-past nine, he dragged through one of the long-
est half-hours that had ever come within his experience.   The captain grew sleepy, Miss Betty gave
short and dry answers ; Hans had himself to pro-
vide the conversation—weary, out of temper, unhappy and love-sick as he was.

At last the clock was close upon half-past nine ;
he rose, explaining that he was accustomed to go
early to bed, because he could read best when he
got up at six o'clock.

"Well, well," said the captain, "do you call this
going early to bed?   I assure you I always turn in
at nine o'clock."

Vexation on vexation !   Hans said good-night
hastily, and rushed down-stairs.

The captain accompanied him to the landing,

candle in hand, and called after him cordially, "Good-night—happy to see you again."

"Thanks!" shouted Hans from below; but he vowed in his inmost soul that he would never set foot in that house again.—

—When the old man returned to the parlor, he found his daughter busy opening the windows.

"What are you doing that for?" asked the captain.

"I'm airing the room after him," answered Miss Betty.

"Come, come, Betty, you are really too hard upon him. But I must admit that the young gentleman did not improve upon closer acquaintance. I don't understand young people nowadays."

Thereupon the captain retired to his bedroom, after giving his daughter the usual evening exhortation, "Now don't sit up too long."

When she was left alone, Miss Betty put out the lamp, moved the flowers away from the corner window, and seated herself on the window-sill with her feet upon a chair.

On clear moonlight evenings she could descry a little strip of the fiord between two high houses. It was not much; but it was a glimpse of the great highway that leads to the south, and to foreign lands.

And her desires and longings flew away, following the same course which has wearied the wings of so many a longing—down the narrow fiord to the south, where the horizon is wide, where the heart expands, and the thoughts grow great and daring.

And Miss Betty sighed as she gazed at the little strip of the fiord which she could see between the two high houses.

—-She gave no thought, as she sat there, to Cousin Hans ; but he thought of Miss Schrappe as he passed with hasty steps up the street.

Never had he met a young lady who was less to his taste. The fact that he had been rude to her did not make him like her better. We are not inclined to find those people amiable who have been the occasion of misbehavior on our own part. It was a sort of comfort to him to repeat to himself, "Who would want to marry her ?"

Then his thoughts wandered to the charmer who was to leave town to-morrow. He realized his fate in all its bitterness, and he felt a great longing to pour forth the sorrow of his soul to a friend who could understand him.

But it was not easy to find a sympathetic friend at that time of night.

After all, Uncle Frederick was his confidant in many matters ; he would look him up.

As he knew that Uncle Frederick was at Aunt Maren's, he betook himself towards the Palace in order to meet him on his way back from Homan's Town. He chose one of the narrow avenues on the right, which he knew to be his uncle's favorite route ; and a little way up the hill he seated himself on a bench to wait.

It must be unusually lively at Aunt Maren's to

make Uncle Frederick stop there until after ten. At last he seemed to discern a small white object far up the avenue ; it was Uncle Frederick's white waistcoat approaching.

Hans rose from the bench and said very seriously, " Good-evening !"

Uncle Frederick was not at all fond of meeting solitary men in dark avenues ; so it was a great relief to him to recognize his nephew.

"Oh, is it only you, Hans old fellow ?" he said, cordially. "What are you lying in ambush here for ?"

" I was waiting for you," answered Hans, in a sombre tone of voice.

" Indeed ? Is there anything wrong with you ? Are you ill ?"

" Don't ask me," answered Cousin Hans.

This would at any other time have been enough to call forth a hail-storm of questions from Uncle Frederick.

But this evening he was so much taken up with his own experiences that for the moment he put his nephew's affairs aside.

" I can tell you, you were very foolish," he said, " not to go with me to Aunt Maren's. We have had such a jolly evening, I'm sure you would have enjoyed it. The fact is, it was a sort of farewell party in honor of a young lady who's leaving town to-morrow."

A horrible foreboding seized Cousin Hans.

"What was her name?" he shrieked, gripping his uncle by the arm.

"Ow!" cried his uncle, "Miss Beck."

Then Hans collapsed upon the bench.

But scarcely had he sunk down before he sprang up again, with a loud cry, and drew out of his coat-tail pocket a knubbly little object, which he hurled away far down the avenue.

"What's the matter with the boy?" cried Uncle Frederick, "What was that you threw away?"

"Oh, it was that confounded Blücher," answered Cousin Hans, almost in tears.

—Uncle Frederick scarcely found time to say, "Didn't I tell you to beware of Blücher?" when he burst into an alarming fit of laughter, which last-ed from the Palace Hill far along Upper Fort Street.

THE END.

www.ingramcontent.com/pod-product-compliance
Lightning Source LLC
Chambersburg PA
CBHW030121030726
47498CB00007B/2484